‖‖‖ ‖‖‖‖ ‖ ‖‖‖‖‖ ‖ ‖‖‖‖‖‖‖ ‖‖‖‖

◁ **W9-AKV-597**

"I Thought Maybe We Could Do Something Together."

Turning, Ingrid faced him directly. She blinked, deliberately feigning innocence. "Are you suggesting we play a game or something? We have Parcheesi, Scrabble and Monopoly."

"They all sound wonderful," he murmured as his fingers trailed down the side of her cheek. She raised her eyes to his and was about to speak when he covered her mouth in a warm, intimate kiss that sent an unexpected shudder throughout his whole body. Stunned at his own response, Joel kissed her tenderly on the tip of her nose and nestled her silky head into his shoulder.

"Very nice," he whispered into her hair. "Much better than Monopoly."

JEAN KENT

was an accountant as well as a self-employed businesswoman until four years ago, when she decided to make a career change. After enrolling in a creative writing class, she dusted off her typewriter and went to work. A resident of Uniontown, Ohio, she has three grown children who lend her encouragement and much-needed support.

Dear Reader:

Romance readers have been enthusiastic about Silhouette Special Editions for years. And that's not by accident: Special Editions were the first of their kind and continue to feature realistic stories with heightened romantic tension.

The longer stories, sophisticated style, greater sensual detail and variety that made Special Editions popular are the same elements that will make you want to read book after book.

We hope that you enjoy this Special Edition today, and will enjoy many more.

The Editors at Silhouette Books

JEAN
KENT
Love's
Advocate

Silhouette Special Edition

Published by Silhouette Books New York

America's Publisher of Contemporary Romance

SILHOUETTE BOOKS
300 E. 42nd St., New York, N.Y. 10017

Copyright © 1985 by Jean Kent

Distributed by Pocket Books

All rights reserved, including the right to reproduce
this book or portions thereof in any form whatsoever.
For information address Silhouette Books,
300 E. 42nd St., New York, N.Y. 10017

ISBN: 0-373-09237-7

First Silhouette Books printing May, 1985

10 9 8 7 6 5 4 3 2 1

All of the characters in this book are fictitious. Any resem-
blance to actual persons, living or dead, is purely coincidental.

Map by Ray Lundgren

SILHOUETTE, SILHOUETTE SPECIAL EDITION and
colophon are registered trademarks of the publisher.

America's Publisher of Contemporary Romance

Printed in the U.S.A.

BC91

To Carol

Love's Advocate

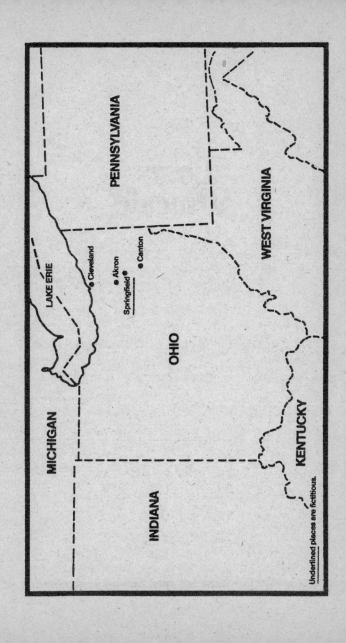

Chapter One

The wind was starting to pick up again, swirling snow across the windshield of the heavy pickup truck in great gusts. Ingrid, tense, sat behind the wheel, leaning forward, all senses alert, her eyes darting from the side of the road to the median strip, to the rearview mirror and forward again. Though it was still midafternoon, there was almost no traffic on the road at all, and for Interstate 77, one of the main arteries into Cleveland, this was almost unheard of.

Finally Ingrid saw the green-and-white exit sign she'd been waiting for: AKRON-CANTON AIRPORT NEXT RIGHT. "Oh, thank God," she said out loud as she felt herself relaxing. She'd traveled this road hundreds of times in all kinds of weather, but even with a three-quarter-ton pickup truck Ohio blizzards were real bears.

Carefully, Ingrid maneuvered the truck around the exit curve and headed straight into the airport, which was separated from the freeway by a large expanse of open fields where the wind was so strong it would have blown a smaller car right off the road. Ingrid's bright, canary-yellow truck, however, drove through the swirling snow like a bulldozer.

Ignoring all No PARKING signs, Ingrid stopped directly in front of the main door of the airport, barely noting that hers was the only vehicle in sight. With a quick look in her rearview mirror, she tucked a wayward strand of dark hair under her red knit cap, tightened the matching scarf around her throat and tugged down the cuffs of her parka. Then, opening the door, she jumped down into a drift of snow that came almost to the tops of her boots. Ingrid, who had spent the entire twenty-eight years of her life in Ohio, was accustomed to snowy winters and, almost casually, she slammed the door behind her and kicked her way through the standing snow and through the main doors into the airport.

Immediately a great big burly man strode up to her. "It's about time you got here!" he stated loudly.

Ingrid gave him a long, narrow look and stamped the snow from her boots with more thump than was necessary. She knew who he was, of course. The great Joel Stires, criminal lawyer extraordinaire, who was the guest speaker at Mount Traver University's weekend seminar. He was also going to be her passenger for a few short miles.

Tugging her cap farther down over her ears, she

raised her dark brown eyes to his blue ones with cool indifference. "For your information, Mr. Stires, you're lucky I got here at all. In case you haven't noticed, it's not exactly a summer day out there."

"I realize that. After all, I've been pacing up and down this damn airport for two hours. Don't you think I can see out the window?"

Ingrid found the condescending tone of his voice maddening. "You're lucky anyone came at all in weather like this," she said. "There's already a foot of snow on the ground, and it's still coming down. Furthermore . . ."

"Look, lady," he interrupted. "I was invited to speak at this seminar. I didn't beg to come. Therefore it seems to me that someone at Mount Traver would have had enough foresight to realize that a snowstorm in Ohio in January was not unforeseeable."

"As far as I'm concerned, they should have had enough foresight to cancel the whole thing." She looked straight at him, her dark eyes snapping. "Permanently."

For the barest moment Ingrid thought she saw a flicker of amusement cross his face, but she wasn't sure. The only thing she was sure of were clear blue eyes that gleamed like bits of glass from the strong masculine face. He was really quite good-looking . . . six-footish, broad, sturdy and blatantly male. Football material, she thought. The kind of man women fawned over, grasping for any crumb of encouragement he might throw their way. And he knew it.

While Ingrid was summing him up, she realized he

was doing a little appraising of his own. After taking in
her knee boots, jeans, heavy jacket and snow cap, he
let his eyes rove across her full face, her rosy cheeks,
her small, upturned nose and down to the curve of her
lips, where they rested for a moment too long. It made
her feel slightly uncomfortable, and she felt compelled
to shift her gaze from his. Surely he wasn't trying to
make a pass at her, was he? And surely the strange
inner excitement she felt was due to her anxiety about
the storm outside and not the nearness of this great bull
of a man before her . . . wasn't it?

As if sensing the disturbance going on inside her, he
seemed to relax slightly, and even managed a small
smile. He was probably on familiar territory. "What's
the matter?" he asked. "Don't you approve of criminal
lawyers?"

His voice brought her back to reality, and once again
Ingrid Christian was in charge of Ingrid Christian. She
squared her shoulders. "Not at the price you charge."

"Oh? You think my fees are exorbitant?" There was
a challenging note in his voice that Ingrid couldn't
resist.

"They are for Mount Traver University," she stated
firmly. "I'm an art teacher there and believe me, our
department could have stretched the money they paid
you a long, long way."

"If you want quality, you pay for it."

"My point exactly. We could have had all the art
reference books in the library rebound in Moroccan
leather for what they paid you."

He tried to suppress a smile. "But it would never

have been as interesting . . ." The sensuous implication was so obvious it was funny. Even Ingrid had to smile.

Clicking her tongue, she shook her head and raised her eyes heavenward. "Oh God," she murmured and, flicking her scarf over her shoulder, she started across the corridor toward the airline counter.

Joel was right behind her. "Where are you going?"

"I have other business here," she explained patiently.

"What other business?" There was a note of incredulity in his voice that brought a smile to Ingrid's lips.

"I hate to tell you, Mr. Stires, but the real purpose of my trip is to pick up a dog. It's only incidental that I agreed to drop you off at the Randolph Inn. In fact, the only reason I agreed to do that was as a favor to a friend."

"Oh, I see," he said, nodding and trying to look rebuffed, but there was no hiding the quirk at the corner of his mouth. For some reason, Mr. Stires was enjoying himself immensely.

And, strangely, so was Ingrid. Despite her opposition to him as a speaker, she had to admit he had a certain charm. Of course, that didn't alter her opinion. If the money Mount Traver had spent on his fee could have gone to the library, thousands of students and local citizens would have benefited. As it was, only two hundred law students would hear him speak and half of those would sleep through the whole lecture.

Ingrid turned her attention to the ticket agent, keeping her back to Joel as much as possible. There was something in the way he kept looking at her that was very unnerving, even when he was standing behind her.

"I hope the airport isn't closed in," she said to the agent. "I'm expecting a dog on that four o'clock plane coming in from Indianapolis."

"Ah, so you're the one," he said. "We were wondering what we were going to do with your pooch if you didn't show up. It came in two hours ago. They couldn't land in Detroit, so they came straight here. Good thing, too, because we're closed now, and so is Pittsburgh. By morning they expect the whole northeast section of the country to be snowed in."

"I guess I just made it under the wire, then," she said. "Now all I have to do is get out of here."

"How far do you have to go?"

"Forty miles due south."

"Whew!" The ticket agent whistled. "You'd better get moving!"

"Right!" came the voice from behind her. "Now where's that dog? Could you bring him out here? We're in a hurry."

The ticket agent looked at the paper Ingrid had given him, then up at Joel. "I'll be right back, Mr."—He glanced down—"Christian."

Ingrid burst out laughing. "That's what you get for butting into my business."

Joel Stires, however, wasn't the least miffed about the mistaken name. With a grin and a shrug of surrender, he held out his hand. Without hesitation, Ingrid put her gloved hand into his open palm, and instantly his fingers closed in a tight grip. She wasn't surprised at the strength or even the warmth of the grasp, but she was startled at the sudden tingling sensation that ran up her arm. Why was it that his handshake seemed more like an invitation than a casual greeting?

His eyes moved across the planes of her face. "You seem to have an unfair advantage. You know who I am, but . . ."

"I'm Ingrid Christian," she interjected quickly. "My friend, Peter Moggs, knew I was coming up here this afternoon to pick up the dog, and he asked me if I'd mind dropping you off at the Randolph Inn. Peter is strictly a fair-weather driver."

He peered at her from beneath his heavy brows. "I'm glad to hear that."

Ingrid felt herself shift uneasily. Normally she would have taken the statement for what it was, a casual compliment, one any man would feel almost obligated to make. But Joel made it sound different, as if he really meant it. Inclining her head in a silent thank you, Ingrid turned her attention back to the counter, and though outwardly she showed great patience, there was no denying the ripple of excitement running through her. But that was only normal, she told herself. Joel Stires was a very attractive man. Any woman would feel a response to him, even if she was a twenty-eight-year-old widow who was more interested in promoting the fine arts than she was in the charm of a strange man.

Joel expelled a long breath and, leaning his back against the counter, stared out into the empty airport with the blank gaze of the patient commuter. It seemed so unlike him that Ingrid couldn't resist sliding a glance in his direction. In profile he was an interesting study. His thick, sandy-brown hair fell across his forehead as if stubbornly defiant, a quality that was repeated in the straight line of his prominent eyebrows, his wide cheekbones and his square, bulldog chin. The total picture was one of strong handsomeness, obstinacy, assertiveness and a generous portion of provocative interest. A very compelling presence, indeed, she mused.

Suddenly his eyes shifted to catch her staring at him. Ingrid quickly averted her gaze and pretended to be absorbed in the snowstorm that still swirled past the windows. Joel let his eyes rest on her for an extra beat, then his gaze followed hers.

"How bad are the roads, anyway?" he asked.

Ingrid shook her head. "Terrible."

"Are we going to have any trouble getting out of here?"

"Probably."

He nodded once. "I appreciate your brevity, but would you mind telling me how you're planning to get through forty miles of this stuff?"

"I have a three-quarter-ton pickup with a four-wheel drive. I can get through anything."

"I see." Once again his boldly assessing glance swept down the full length of her body. Even in her heavy winter clothing, Ingrid was strikingly attractive. The planes of her face, from the pronounced cheekbones to the angular slant of her chin, were clearly defined. Though her features showed a classic strength, nothing could conceal her femininity. She had lustrous dark eyes, long black lashes and a graceful way of moving, like a branch bending and swaying in the wind.

The ticket agent returned and shoved a heavy, cardboard dog carrier across the metal counter. The case wiggled impatiently, and Ingrid leaned over to peer through the round opening at the end. She was immediately rewarded by a wet tongue on her cheek.

"Oh, isn't she adorable?" she cooed to no one in particular.

"A real spectacle," Joel said as he grabbed the handle of the crate and started for the door. "Let's go."

"No! Wait a minute." Ingrid yanked at his sleeve. "I want to take her out of the crate."

With a weary sigh, he set the crate down on the floor and glanced meaningfully at his watch. "We're in a hurry . . . or at least we should be."

Ingrid tossed the remark aside and, dropping to her knees, began to unfasten the crate with hurried fingers. Within minutes she was cuddling a little black bundle of energy that was so delighted to get out of the box it wouldn't keep still. But Ingrid managed to nuzzle the little dog into her neck and soothe it with soft, purring murmurs.

"That thing's screwy," came the comment from above.

"Well, what do you expect?" she retorted defensively. "She's been cooped up in that crate for over four hours."

"Hmmm." Joel studied the little, fat dog with a critical eye. "In my opinion, it looks more like a pig than a dog."

Ingrid shot him a cold glare and gave the dog another loving pat. "I don't remember asking for your opinion."

Evidently her passenger felt obligated to apologize, and well he should. "I didn't mean to insult you. It's just that I'm from the city. I've never seen a pig before. I thought that's what they looked like."

Ingrid couldn't help it. She found herself mellowing. Here was a man accustomed to getting himself out of tight spots. He did a pretty good job of it, too, she thought, as she shoved her jeans' cuffs deeper into her boots, pulled on her gloves, picked up the dog and turned to Joel Stires. "Ready?" she asked with a lift of her brows.

"I have to get my luggage."

"Well, hurry up. We have to get going."

"I won't be a minute," he promised, then bolted across the airport and around the corner to the baggage pickup area.

Ingrid decided to take the chance to visit the ladies' room. Tucking the dog under her arm, she pushed through the door marked WOMEN. As it swung shut behind her, she could hear an exasperated groan of protest from the visiting speaker. Men were such boors, she thought and, putting the dog down, she inspected her with an appreciative eye. She was a beautiful specimen of a French bulldog; flat ribs, sloping croup, plump body, flanks drawn up and, even more important, she had a good disposition. It was hard for Ingrid to resist playing with her, but time was awasting.

Adjusting her cap, which completely covered her long, dark hair, Ingrid inspected herself in the mirror. Leaning forward a little, she smoothed her eyebrows back with a long, delicate finger. The eyes that stared back at her were large and dark brown and shining with an inner sparkle that hadn't been there in a long time. Her cheeks were flushed, too, and her lips seemed curved in a permanent smile. She looked positively vivacious. Must be the weather, she tried to convince herself. Then, with a final nod to the image in the mirror, she squared her shoulders, picked up the dog and walked out into the corridor.

Her passenger was leaning insolently against a post, his lips drawn into a line of exaggerated impatience. At his feet was the largest suitcase she had ever seen.

"I hope you realize that thing has to ride in back in the open truck bed."

"Under two feet of snow? Not on your life. All my winter stuff is in there."

"Look, Mr. Stires, this is not an airport limousine. It's a pickup truck. It doesn't have a backseat or even an enclosed trunk."

He wasn't to be daunted. "I'm very familiar with the appearance of a pickup truck. I also happen to know there's a space behind the front seat that would easily accommodate this suitcase."

"That space happens to be filled with my gear," she informed him coolly.

"Gear? What kind of gear?"

"Well," she answered vaguely, "there are boots and

a blanket and a tire iron and two boxes of art supplies and my library books and . . ."

"We'll manage," he interrupted. "Now what do you say we get going?"

Without waiting for an answer, he grabbed his suitcase with one hand and her arm with the other and hustled her toward the door. Ingrid had never felt so manipulated in her life, but she didn't bother to voice an objection. After all, ten miles down the road she'd be rid of him forever.

They paused a moment in the vestibule while Ingrid tugged on her gloves. The truck, which she'd parked right in front of the airport's main entrance, was covered with snow.

"Ready?" he asked.

Nodding, she tightened her grip on the dog, then swung her eyes over Joel's broad frame. He wore his clothes loosely, as though his muscles needed more room than the confines of a well-tailored suit allowed. He was wearing leather executive boots and a knee-length coat open from throat to hem. No hat. No gloves. No scarf.

"You're not exactly dressed for a snowstorm," she noted.

"I'll manage."

"But the windchill factor out here is probably twenty below zero. Don't you think you'd better button your coat and turn up your collar?"

Joel dipped his head in a gracious salute. "I'm a big boy now."

"Oh, all right!" Ingrid tossed her head indignantly. "Go ahead and freeze."

Pushing open the door, she ran through the snow, head down, collar up. The wind was fierce and cold, with a sting to it that made her face burn. Plunging through a deep drift, she made her way to the driver's side. Putting the dog down for a moment, she opened the door and crawled across the wide seat to unlock the passenger door. It opened almost immediately.

"Cripes, the windchill factor out here must be twenty degrees below zero," Joel complained, raising his voice above the wind.

Ingrid lifted her eyes skyward, reached for the snow brush and backed out of the truck. Joel had pushed the front seat forward and was shoving her gear around every whichway to find room for his gigantic suitcase. Ingrid could have murdered him on the spot. She was very particular about her things . . . and all this for a lousy ten-minute ride. Why couldn't he have walked, for crying out loud?

Slamming the door with a loud thwack, she started clearing off the windows, not forgetting for a moment that while she was standing out in the freezing blizzard, her passenger was sitting in the truck, safely sheltered from the elements. As she ran the scraper across the windshield, there was an insistent tap on the glass. Mr. Stires was good enough to point out a spot she'd missed. God, he had crust, she thought as she finished the job, picked up the dog and got into the truck.

"I hope you find my work acceptable," she quipped.

"Yes, you did a good job," he assured her, leaning back comfortably in his seat. "But then, I knew you would. You're a very meticulous person."

"How would you know?" she asked as she settled the dog on her blanket.

"Oh, by the neat way you're folding that pink thing around piggy here. Plus," he added, his glance roving over her approvingly, "other observations I've made."

"I don't know what they'd be," she said, digging in her pocket for her keys. She hadn't missed the seductive note in his voice and, for the first time since she'd met him, she found herself relaxing. "You've only known me five minutes."

"It's closer to twenty. And you can learn a lot about a person in twenty minutes."

"Is that right?" Ingrid didn't even have to glance at him to know there was a spark of devilment behind those heavy brows and sensuous mouth. He certainly was taking a lot of liberties for a stranger but, somehow, this seemed to be in keeping with his character. Despite his outspokenness, he had a certain languid charm. She had to admit that he was probably a very good speaker. He not only looked impressive, he could bluff his way through anything. She was beginning to see why the committee had hired him, though she still didn't approve.

His eyes remained on her as she settled herself behind the wheel. "Isn't it a little unusual for a woman your size to own a pickup truck?"

"It was my husband's," she said as she started the engine.

He caught that right away. She knew he would. "Was?" he repeated.

Ingrid knew he was digging, prying into her private life. She should simply say yes, and let that be the end of the discussion, but something deep within her couldn't be stilled.

"I'm a widow," she explained.

"I see." He sat back but his eyes never left her face.

For a moment Ingrid thought she was going to blush and she found herself lowering her eyes, avoiding his gaze. What in the world was wrong with her, anyway? she chastised herself. Since Rob's death a year ago, she hadn't even thought of another man, and here she was physically attracted to a perfect stranger who was as nosy as hell but had enough charisma to get away with his probing questions.

As though sensing the conflicts going on inside her, Joel smiled pleasantly and stretched his arm across the back of her seat, buddy-buddy style. "Well, I guess we have something in common after all. I'm divorced and you're a widow, so that makes us both single, right?"

"I suppose so," she agreed, not quite sure what he meant by that. Was being single a unique bond between two people? Ingrid didn't know. She hadn't been single that long, but something told her she'd be wise to get started and drop off her passenger before she made a total fool of herself.

She revved the engine a little, shifted into low and eased away from the curb. As she angled into the exit lane, she could feel Joel Stires's eyes lingering on her face. Usually she didn't mind a passenger watching her drive, but today it was very disconcerting. She felt compelled to start a conversation, something on safer ground. "This is the worst storm I've seen in years, but if my windshield doesn't freeze up on me, we'll have you tucked into a nice cozy bar in no time."

Joel dipped his head in an assenting nod and, to her relief, turned forward in his seat. "Now what's the name of this motel?"

"It's the Randolph Inn, on Route Thirty-nine. About ten miles from here."

"And you have thirty miles to go from there?"

"Yes, and the last five miles of that is on country roads."

"You live on a farm?" His voice sounded incredulous.

"No. As a matter of fact, I live in the woods."

"The woods?" he repeated thoughtfully. "Hmmm. I don't think I've ever known anyone who lived in the woods."

"It's beautiful there."

"Yes," he nodded, "I suppose it would be." Ingrid could almost see him cataloging the information in his mind, but he made no further comment. Instead, he turned his attention to the road ahead and squinted to see through the windshield. Then, leaning forward in his seat, he peered even closer, as though weighing the possibilities of their survival. And this was understandable. As soon as the canary-yellow truck left the shelter of the terminal, the wind hit them full force. The rear end swayed a little but Ingrid, long experienced in handling a pickup truck on icy roads, drove slowly but steadily through the drifting snow. Straining, she leaned forward, searching for a familiar landmark that would guide her to the entrance ramp of the freeway.

Suddenly Joel tensed and sat up straight. "There's the ramp, over there on your right." He pointed insistently. "Stay over here on this side. Get closer to the curb. This way. A little farther . . ."

"That's not the freeway," she informed him calmly. "That's the cut-off to the rear of the airport. It's up ahead three hundred yards or so."

"Oh, I see," he said, but he didn't relax his vigil for one moment. He kept craning his neck to see better. "There's a row of posts over there half covered with snow," he reported.

"Tell me about it."

"Stop sign coming up. Watch it! Keep to the left."

Ingrid brought the truck to a stop and took a deep breath. "What are the chances of you sitting back and buckling in and leaving the driving to me?" Her voice, though calm, had a steel edge to it. "You're not only blocking my view, you're making me nervous."

"I don't know why you'd say that," he retorted, unimpressed with her stern look. "Two pairs of eyes are better than one."

"Not in this case," she retorted, her temper rising.

His gaze skimmed the length of her body which, despite her bulky clothing, was obviously slender and delicate.

"Are you sure you can handle this hog truck in a snowstorm?"

"It is not a hog truck," she snapped in sudden

defense of her vehicle. "Obviously you don't know beans from backwater about driving in an ice storm. I, however, have done it all my life. Therefore," she added, "I'd appreciate fewer suggestions."

He threw his hands up in the air in a dramatic gesture of defeat. "All right. Have it your way. Run us into a ditch. Get us stuck in a snowdrift. Why not?"

Gritting her teeth, she cast him a glowering look. She was tempted to answer him, but she knew that was exactly what he wanted, and she refused to give him the satisfaction of winning an argument. And win he would. Mr. Stires wasn't the type who'd ever lose one. He'd carry it on endlessly rather than admit defeat, and Ingrid wasn't one who enjoyed a war of words, not that she couldn't give him a run for his money. But at the moment she had other things to do.

Once they got onto the freeway, the going was a little easier, so when the dog stirred slightly, Ingrid reached down to pet it.

Joel's eye caught the motion. "Why don't you keep your hands on the wheel and I'll do the dog patting?"

Ingrid slid him a warning glance. "I can see this is going to be a long ten miles."

"Nevertheless, I'll do the patting, all right?" Immediately he proceeded to tap the dog on the head in a clumsy attempt to soothe it.

It was quite obvious he'd never been around dogs before, and Ingrid couldn't help but wonder what sort of background he had. She'd always thought men and dogs went together. But perhaps he'd lived in the city all his life and thought that pets were something other people owned. This seemed strange to Ingrid, who'd been raised in the country. She couldn't imagine life without animals. Odd, she thought, how two people who had traveled such different paths should touch for a brief moment in time and then separate, perhaps never to meet again.

The dog seemed to be enjoying Joel's ministrations. She raised her little black face up to his, her eyes round and soulful and innocently adoring.

Imitating the dog, Joel squished up his nose. "I think this thing needs a bath," he complained, but Ingrid noticed that he didn't take his hand from her head.

"It's a dog, you know. Not a baby."

"I realize that," he said, "but what I don't understand is why you'd buy a dog from Indiana. Couldn't you have just picked up something locally at the dog pound?"

"Dog pound!" she spluttered indignantly. "I'll have you know this is a French bulldog with a pedigree a mile long. They happen to be very rare in this area, so my brother and I are going to start raising them." She patted the dog again. "And believe me, they don't come cheap."

"How much, if I may be so blunt?"

Ingrid felt that *blunt* was a good word. It seemed to sum up Joel Stires's personality quite well. Normally she'd have resented his prying, but under the circumstances, it didn't really matter. She'd be rid of him in just a few more miles.

"Seven-fifty," she answered.

To Ingrid's surprise, he cocked his head in a gesture

of approval. It was the last thing she'd expected. Scorn and ridicule, yes, but assent?

"That's not bad at all," he stated. "In fact, it's cheap. Even the dog pounds charge ten, don't they?"

"Dog pound!" Ingrid cried again. She shot him a hard, exasperated look. "We are talking about seven hundred and fifty."

If she'd hit him in the face with a snowball, he couldn't have been more stunned, at least outwardly.

"Oh, my God!" he swore, falling back into his seat in a dramatic display of shocked horror. "You can't be serious!"

"I certainly am," she retorted smugly. There, that should shut him up for a few more miles.

A few more miles? Ingrid sat up, instantly alert. And then it was her turn to gasp and fall back into her seat in shocked horror.

"Oh, my God! I've missed the Route Thirty-nine exit ramp!"

Chapter Two

"What?" Joel screeched as he leaned forward in his seat. "You missed the exit ramp? What do you mean you missed it? It's not possible. How could you? I thought you knew this road like the back of your hand . . ."

"Oh, keep quiet," she shouted angrily, biting back tears of frustration. "I'm having enough trouble keeping this damn truck on the road without having to put up with your constant bickering. It's your fault I missed that exit. If you'd been watching instead of playing with the dog . . ."

"But you distinctly told me not to watch."

"I did not. I told you not to make suggestions."

"And to sit back and buckle up," he reminded her.

"I don't know why you couldn't sit back and buckle

up and watch the road at the same time. That doesn't sound like too difficult a chore to me."

"All right. All right," he shouted, raising his hands in the air. "Don't shoot. I give up. It's all my fault. I confess. Now, where in hell is the next exit?"

"About twelve miles," she said through clenched teeth, wondering what she'd done to deserve this punishment in the first place. "And that's not the worst of it. There's no motel there. I'll have to bring you back."

"No motel? I've never heard of an exit without a motel."

"You've never been in rural Ohio."

"You're right, I haven't. And with luck, I never will be again."

"Thanks for the plaudit. I feel the same way about Indiana."

"I'm not from Indiana. I'm from New York. I travel a lot."

The truck suddenly slowed as they hit a stretch of road where the snow had drifted into deep piles. Ingrid struggled to keep the wheels straight as her eyes searched for the edge of the pavement, a sign, a post, anything to indicate she was still on the highway. Finally, by sheer luck, she made it through the drifts, but her anxiety grew as she glanced at the gas gauge. Almost half a tank. Plenty to get her home, but adding another twenty-four miles in this weather to take her passenger back to the motel would be stretching it a little.

"You'd think they'd have the snowplows out by now," he complained. "I mean, it isn't as though Ohio is surprised by this storm, is it?"

"They always wait until the snow stops."

"Great. And what happens if we get stuck?"

"Right now, I'm more worried about the gas than I am about getting stuck. I doubt if any stations will be open, and I'm not sure I have enough."

He looked at the gauge. "What's your tank capacity?"

"I get eleven miles to the gallon."

"That's not what I asked."

"That's the only statistic I know regarding this vehicle," she snapped irritably, her frayed nerves strained to the limit.

"It seems to me you'd—whoa!"

The front end took a sudden slide to the right. Ingrid turned into the skid, straightened the wheels and brought the truck back on the road. Wearily, she shifted in her seat. Her arms and shoulders were beginning to stiffen with fatigue and tension, and she could feel the beginnings of a headache behind her eyes.

The snow was coming so fast now that the wipers couldn't keep up with the onslaught and left streaks of ice on the windshield. Fortunately, she knew every dip and curve in the road and even without the edge of the shoulder to guide her, she knew she could get through somehow. Adding twenty-four miles onto the trip, however, especially with darkness coming so soon, worried her. She wondered if it also worried her passenger. She was very much aware of him watching her, but he didn't seem to be anxious. It was more as though he was studying her, trying to determine just what pigeonhole she'd fit into. Ingrid found herself wondering what sort of woman he was accustomed to. Probably the glittering, show-girl type. He seemed to be a man who needed a lot of attention.

Out of the corner of her eye, Ingrid could see that he'd completed his perusal of her and had turned to face forward again. She couldn't resist a quick glance at his profile, outlined now against the dark shadows of the landscape. The forehead was broad, the nose straight, the jaw set with a permanently determined look. The whole picture was one of bulldog tenacity. Ingrid could see that he'd make a big impression on a jury. His bright, keen eyes, his massive figure and deep, authoritative voice would easily capture and hold his audience. Furthermore, he would know his subject well and deal with it in a cold, logical manner. He'd be blunt and direct, stating the bare facts without embellishments . . . or would he? she wondered, remembering his flair for the dramatic and its subsequent results. Even Ingrid was finding him to be one of the most fascinating men she'd ever met.

"I have a suggestion to make," Joel said, breaking a long silence.

Ingrid came instantly alert. "What's that?"

Spacing his words carefully, he spoke with the conviction and authority of an experienced trial lawyer who was trying to win over a jury. "As you can see, it's getting dark. If you have to take me back to the motel, that will add another twenty-four miles to your trip. You don't have enough gas or time or"—his eyes swept down the length of her parka—"energy for that. Therefore"—she could almost see those blue eyes flicker—"I don't think you should turn back. I can spend the night at your place."

Ingrid blinked, stunned. Had she heard right?

"Would you mind repeating that?"

He stretched his long legs out before him in a remarkably relaxed position and folded his arms across his chest. He had reached a decision. "I'll spend the night at your place. Surely you have a spare cot or something. Everyone does."

"They do?" she asked numbly.

"And tomorrow morning someone from Mount Traver can pick me up and take me to the conference."

He sounded as if everything was all settled, but she noticed his eyes flicking in her direction as he assessed her response. Her immediate reaction, once she got over the initial shock, was a firm negative.

Sensing this, Joel hurried on before Ingrid could get a word out. "I should be out of there first thing in the morning. By tomorrow at this time I'll be on my way back to New York."

"Hmmm."

Ingrid had to think about that for a moment. The suggestion was certainly practical, and it involved such a short period of time that it seemed petty for Ingrid to object. And, of course, she did have a spare bedroom. Two of them, in fact. But living alone as she did, was it wise to invite this strange man to be her houseguest? Not that she really thought he'd make a pass at her if she objected—but would she object?

Ingrid shook herself. What a ridiculous thought. Just because Joel Stires was impressive in appearance and had been watching her out of the corner of his eye the whole ride and had reminded her that they were both single, didn't mean there was a romantic interest for either of them. Besides, the idea of his staying overnight did have merits. In the long run she'd be safer at home with Joel Stires than out here on the highway for another hour.

"I suppose it would be all right," she found herself saying, "but I can't guarantee the . . ."

"Never mind the guarantees." He waved impatiently. "Let's just get there."

"Sounds good to me," she said, suddenly relieved.

For the barest moment Ingrid saw Joel's depthless eyes blink, then slowly slide away from her face. Even in the dim light she could see that he was trying hard to control a smile of triumph. She shook her head. His air of superiority was exasperating, but she had to admit it was also provocative. In fact, everything about Joel Stires added up to a very interesting man. And an attractive one, too. Even Ingrid had to admit that every time his eyes swept down the length of her body, she felt her pulse skip a beat, but all women were like that. They loved to dream up dashing heroes and romantic situations. Nothing ever came of their dreams, of course, and they never expected it to. Still, Ingrid had to admit that having the handsome Joel Stires spend the night at her house came close . . .

They drove a little way in silence. Joel shifted in his seat, moving a little closer to the dog who shared the space between them. It was dark now and Ingrid drove with the headlights on. Though her view was restricted considerably, so was Joel's. He had nothing to look at except the interior of the truck.

Turning toward her, he stretched his arm across the back of the seat. "How old is your brother?" he asked suddenly.

"Seventeen. Why?"

"Just wondered. Does he live with you?"

"No, he lives with my parents. They live only about five miles from me."

"Is yours a close-knit family?"

"Yes, but not obsessively so. We actually do more telephoning than visiting."

He nodded in understanding, but he didn't say any more. Ingrid resisted the impulse to ask him about his family. Probably he had been born and raised in the city, where he'd learned to deal with adverse situations on any level.

Finally, they turned onto County Road 212, just one mile from home. The truck moved silently through the world of white castles that surrounded them. A world where Ingrid had grown up accepting the buffeting winds of time but never losing sight of the magnificent splendor of the wooded hills and fields that shaped her life just as the wind had shaped the oaks and maples around her.

Joel remained strangely silent. Ingrid found herself wondering what a man who had never known the wonders of nature thought about. Would his world, by necessity, be a cold and calculating one? It would seem so to her, yet from the little she knew of Joel Stires, she was beginning to think a lot of his arrogance and pushiness was pure theatrics. Perhaps it was a convenient cover for one whose reputation as a criminal lawyer had to be tough and unyielding. She was sure that if she could look beneath that hard-boiled exterior, she would find a man who was compassionate and understanding and might even be swayed into thinking French bulldogs made wonderful pets and were well worth any price. Ingrid had to tuck her chin into the collar of her coat to hide her smile. She realized she was getting tired—so tired, in fact, that she was beginning to get silly.

Suddenly she braked, bringing the truck almost to a stop.

Joel jerked forward. "What's the matter?"

She pointed to the side of the road. "Deer."

"What?"

"Deer." The headlights picked up the luminous glow of eyes in the dark. She pointed again. "Over there in the thicket. I'm afraid they might run out in front of the truck."

He peered through the windshield, all senses alert,

and bobbed his head back and forth until, finally, he saw them. "I can hardly make them out."

"They're masters of camouflage, all right. That and their speed are their only defenses."

"How did you see them?"

"All animals have eyes that shine in the dark."

"But how did you know it was deer?" he argued. "It could have been a cat or something."

She blinked, disbelieving. "Five feet tall?"

"Oh," he murmured, "I hadn't thought of that."

She started up again, slower this time, her eyes sweeping the sides of the road for any signs of wildlife. Just before they turned into the long drive leading up to the cedar-sided ranch house, a rabbit scurried across the road and disappeared into the night. Joel stared in amazement at the departing animal.

"Cat," Ingrid explained.

"I knew that!"

They turned toward each other simultaneously and burst out laughing. The sudden release of tension after the long trip left them both feeling lighthearted and a little giddy. Ingrid found herself delighting in the shared triumph, something she had missed for a long while. Shifting the truck into low gear, she started up the drive that led to the house at the top of the slope. When the truck finally rolled to a stop at the rear of the building, she expelled a long-held sigh of relief. And so did Joel.

Turning to her, he dipped his head in a salute and grinned broadly. "My compliments to the driver."

Smiling, Ingrid inclined her head in a graceful bow. "Thank you. I deserved that."

For a moment their eyes caught and held in a look that wiped away all the animosity between them and left in its place a disturbing awareness. Ingrid, sensing that Joel was willing to carry their newfound compatibility one step farther, quickly averted her gaze. Switching off the engine, she busied herself taking the keys out of the ignition and stuffing them in her pocket. All the while, Joel watched with that inscrutable expression of his that sent a shiver trembling down her spine. Despite all his blustering, he was a man very much attuned to the opposite sex. Even in the dark she could see his expressive eyes studying her face.

Suddenly Ingrid realized she was sitting in the truck, lost in some faraway reverie, while the storm outside swirled around them in icy gusts. Tugging her cap down again and pulling on her gloves, she picked up the dog and put her hand on the door handle. Then she turned to Joel, who appeared to be perfectly content to sit there forever.

"Ready?" she asked.

"Always," was the quick reply.

Without stopping to analyze that, Ingrid opened the door and jumped to the ground. She couldn't help but pause to look around her. As far as the eye could see, everything was covered with snow. It was like walking into wonderland, and no matter how many times Ingrid had seen it, each trip was as beautiful and awesome as the first one.

Putting the dog down in the snow, she turned to help

Joel with his luggage, but he'd already retrieved it and was walking around the front of the truck to meet her. To Ingrid's surprise, he took her arm and led her up the walk as if he were ushering her into his house instead of the other way around. Oh, well, she thought, he was simply the takeover type, and there was absolutely nothing she could do about it, short of declaring war.

The dog followed in their footsteps as they hurried to the house, the wind at their backs.

"Aren't you afraid that pup will freeze?" Joel shouted as a gust of snow swirled around them.

Ingrid shook her head. "No. French bulldogs are a hearty breed. Besides, she's not a pup. She's two years old."

He nodded, accepting her explanation, then slowed his pace as the trees suddenly parted and the large, rambling ranch house stretched across the landscape like a giant sleeping in the snow. He looked so stunned that Ingrid realized he had expected to see the conventional ranch-type house that inundated all of suburban America. But Tawny, the name Ingrid had given the house when it was built six years before, was an architectural masterpiece. Long, low and sprawling, with a slightly elevated central section, it blended into its surroundings with casual elegance. Huge picture windows, sliding glass doors and open-air porches testified to the uniqueness of its design and beauty. It was one of the few material things in the world that Ingrid loved.

They entered through a heavy oak door that opened into a small room with a stone floor, white brick walls and a wide-beamed ceiling. As Joel stamped the snow from his feet, he looked around him, his brows raised in an expression of pleasant surprise.

"What is this? The utility room?" he asked as he started unbuttoning his coat.

"No, that's on the other side of the kitchen," Ingrid said, tossing her gloves onto a weathered table. "I call this the snow room in winter and the garden room in summer." Removing her parka, she threw it onto a wall hook and started pulling off her boots.

Joel followed suit, but his eyes were on his surroundings. "Looks like an old English pub. Is the rest of the house as unusual as this?"

"More or less," she said as she started pulling a heavy sweater over her head. "I drew sketches of what I considered the ideal country house, and my husband gave them to an architect who, of course, had to revise a lot of things to make them feasible." Her cap had come off with her sweater. Long strands of silky black hair fell across her cheeks and forehead. She pushed them back, unconscious of the captivating picture she made as she stood before him in her stocking feet, tight jeans and a white knit top that clung to her body, accentuating the soft curves of her breasts. "I'm mad about English architecture," she went on. "I wanted a Tudor, but they're too formal for this part of the country, so I settled for my own version."

Joel watched, fascinated, until her last outer garment had been removed. With both hands, she pushed her hair away from her face and looked up at him. Her cheeks were flushed from the wind, her eyes sparkling with an inner glow of happiness. Joel scanned her willowy frame with such frank approval that Ingrid couldn't resist nodding a polite thank you. It'd been a long time since a man had noticed her . . . wrong—since she had noticed a man. Clearing her throat, Ingrid hastily led the way down a corridor to the main part of the house.

Joel walked beside her, so close she could feel his jacket brushing lightly against her arm. When they paused in the elaborately tiled foyer, she stepped a little to one side. "I'll show you where your room is," she said. "You might want to change into something less formal than that business suit."

"You have a point," he agreed. "Wait a minute. I'll get my gear."

Joel went back to the snow room and returned, hefting the large suitcase easily in one hand. To Ingrid, it looked like it weighed a ton.

"I'll say one thing, you don't believe in traveling light."

"That's because I've spent the last four days with a friend who thinks he's located an oil drilling site and is trying to find ten people to invest in it."

"Ah," Ingrid nodded, understanding. "Then you probably spent two days tramping through the snow and another day pouring over geologists' reports."

Joel looked surprised. "How did you know?"

"My husband was an oil geologist," she explained as they crossed the carpeted salon to the west wing of the house. "Believe me, we've had many meetings here where every tenth word was either 'oil' or 'gas.' "

"I know. You get caught up in it. It's a compulsion once you've been exposed." She saw him swing a sideways glance in her direction. "Sometimes people affect you that way, too. They're so interesting and you get so caught up in them that they dominate every thought." His eyes bore down on her. "Don't you agree?"

Ingrid felt a tingling sensation and inadvertently rubbed her arm with her hand as if to put a stop to it. "Yes, I suppose," she murmured, trying to appear as unconcerned as possible. This was no time to get started on that.

Opening the door into a large, nicely furnished bedroom, she switched on the lights and went over to the windows to close the drapes. When she turned around, Joel was watching her with an expression that combined amusement with curiosity. Setting his suitcase just inside the room, he peered at the closed door across the hall.

"Is that your room?" he asked casually. Too casually.

Ingrid was quick to set him straight. "No, it's not," she informed him firmly. "My room is on the other side of the house. This is the guest wing."

He glanced out into the hall. "Three guest rooms? You must do a lot of entertaining."

"We did quite a bit when my husband was alive, but even then these rooms were seldom used." Almost wistfully, she glanced around the room. "Actually, when we built the house, this was supposed to be the children's wing."

"I see." He nodded solemnly. "You must have expected to have a large family."

"Yes, we'd planned on three children, but, well, things just didn't turn out that way." She sighed resignedly. "At first we were both so career oriented that we decided to wait, and then Rob had a heart attack . . ." Her voice trailed off uncertainly.

"And you decided it was too late," he finished.

"No, we decided to wait a little longer. Starting a family would have put too much strain on him."

"I can understand that," he nodded, "but it's not too late for you, Ingrid. You're still young; you have your whole life ahead of you."

"Yes, I know. In fact, I keep telling myself that all the time, but . . ."

"But at the moment, there's no man in the picture?"

His not-so-subtle prodding brought a smile to Ingrid's face. "No, there isn't," she admitted, "but there *are* other things in the picture and one of them is to get you settled in while I call my brother and tell him the dog arrived safe and sound." It was time to get this conversation back onto an impersonal level, she told herself, and in three long strides she crossed the room toward the door. But Joel was standing in the doorway, almost completely filling the frame, and he made no effort to make room for her to pass.

"Pardon me," she murmured.

"Hmmm?"

Ingrid slid him a knowing glance. "Never mind the 'hmmm.' Just get out of the way."

Joel straightened as though suddenly realizing the situation. "Oh, of course," he said quickly. He shuffled his feet and shifted his weight and turned his shoulders. Still, when he was all through, he was still blocking the doorway.

Ingrid sighed audibly, but she found it hard to keep from smiling. Evidently his crafty maneuvering didn't end in the courtroom. Undaunted, Ingrid squeezed past him, her body lightly brushing against his. She was aware of him watching her, assessing her. Quickly Ingrid sidled out of the room and hurried down the hall.

Retreating to the sanctuary of her own room, Ingrid took a moment to sit down on the edge of her bed and try to sort out her reactions to Joel Stires. When she had first met him at the airport, she'd thought he represented everything she disliked in a man. He was not only quick-tempered and pushy, but he was quick to criticize and condemn, a fault finder who trusted no one but himself. And yet there was an understanding, an unexpected gentleness, which he was careful to conceal. Strangely, she found herself wondering if he had ever yearned for something he couldn't have. Had he known tears and bitter disappointment and despair? Or had he been able to bypass all that in his reach for the ultimate goal—power.

With an uncertain shake of her head, Ingrid turned her attention to undressing. Her jeans were damp from melted snow and her knit top suddenly seemed plain and unattractive. She yearned to take a nice, long, soaking bath, but she knew her guest would probably be pacing the floor if left alone for more than a few minutes. She decided to settle for a face scrub and, going into the bathroom, she switched on the lights, flooding the huge room with color.

Ingrid's bathroom, or bathing room, as it was technically referred to, was a spectacular break with convention. Contradictory to the old-English decor of the rest of the house, it definitely leaned toward the modern Japanese in design, but was so unique that even now, after six years, it held Ingrid spellbound. One whole wall of the huge room was thermo-paned from floor to ceiling so that anyone relaxing in the immense circular tub could feast their eyes on a gorgeous view of the countryside. Framing the tub were weeping fig trees, giant philodendron, schefflera and hanging ivy. Around the tub were pots of assorted tropical plants. The result was that it looked more like a spa than a bathroom, and Ingrid loved every inch of it.

Her luxurious bath, however, would have to wait until tomorrow, after Joel had gone to the seminar and she had the house to herself. In the meantime, she tackled the decision of what to wear. Despite her country life-style, Ingrid loved exotic clothes. Her husband had encouraged it, often buying expensive robes and slacks when he was away on a trip, and Ingrid always delighted in dressing up when she was home. Selecting a lounge suit of deep amber and orange velour, she started putting it on, but paused a moment to reconsider. Under the circumstances, was it a little too dressy? perhaps even provocative? She didn't want Joel Stires to get the impression that she was a siren out to snag herself a man. On the other hand, the suit was one of her favorite snowy-night outfits. It was warm and comfortable and the rich color, which most people found impossible to wear, made her skin glow and put lights in her eyes. Besides, she argued with herself, why should she let any man make the decision for her? If you want to wear it, Ingrid, put it on. Quit worrying about what Joel will think. Just because he's attractive and attentive and as arrogant as the storm outside doesn't mean you have to go around in sackcloth and ashes.

As Ingrid turned from side to side, looking at herself in the mirror, she had to admit she looked rather elegant, and realized this was the first time since Rob's death that she had felt like dressing up, an encouraging sign. Avoiding bright colors and exotic fabrics, she'd lounged around in jeans and cotton shirts for the past year. But no more, she thought, and with a determined lift of her chin, Ingrid tugged down her sleeves, fastened the belt and looped a gold-beaded chain about her neck. She looked sumptuous and she felt sumptuous, and if Joel Stires got the wrong impression, she'd set him straight pronto. No more drab colors for her.

Chapter Three

Joel's bedroom was connected to the second guest room by a bath that had a very large shower stall, snow-white towels and a warm, thick rug. The invitation was irresistible.

Joel, always neat with his clothes, opened the closet door for a hanger for his business suit and immediately spied a child's lamp on the shelf. Its base was a ceramic horse poised on his hind legs with his head thrown back, his front hooves clawing the air, his mane flying in wild abandon. Surprised, even stunned, Joel dropped his suit onto the nearest chair and, lifting the lamp from the shelf, carefully turned it over in his hands. It was exactly like a lamp he'd had when he was a child. Had it been Ingrid's? he wondered. Probably. It would be so like her to save it all these years to give to her child one day.

Setting it down on the dresser, Joel removed the bulb from the bedside reading light, screwed it into the child's lamp and turned it on. It worked beautifully and looked absolutely magnificent. He stood back, a little in awe. It had been thirty years since he'd seen his lamp, but he remembered it as clearly as if it had been yesterday. It had been a gift from his grandmother on his sixth birthday.

He could never remember Gran Stires being well. It seemed to Joel as a child that she was always sick with something, but he never remembered her going to the doctor. She lived with her son, Joel's father, and his wife and son in a huge three-story house in northeastern Oklahoma. His father, an ambitious man whose interests included wheat farming, real estate sales, horse trading and gas and oil drilling, made a lot of money. He also spent a lot, giving his family whatever they asked for. There seemed to be no limit to his generosity, but there was a limit to the time he spent at home. When Nat Stires got involved in drilling a new well, days, sometimes weeks would go by when Joel didn't see him.

Since they had been a lifetime habit, his absences didn't bother Joel at all. Evidently they bothered his mother, though. When Joel was nine, she kissed him good-bye, got into the car and drove off with some man Joel had never seen before. At first he had been puzzled, then angry, and then he had forgotten about it. He had never known his mother very well anyway, and as long as Gran was there, his needs were satisfied.

And she was always there, ready to read a book or

tell him a story or give advice or just listen to a young boy's dreams, as well as his complaints.

"When's Dad coming home, anyway? He said he'd bring me an airplane with a real motor in it that could fly right across the lawn to Henderson's yard."

"Your dad's a busy man. He has to make a lot of money to support a place like this," Gran would always remind him.

"Is it hard to make money, Gran?"

"Oh, yes, very hard. Only the smartest and the strongest survive."

"I'm smart and strong. I'm going to be a millionaire."

"That's very nice, Joel. Your dad will be very proud of you if you're a millionaire. But remember," she said, gently stroking his hair with her long fingers, "don't forget to stop and smell the flowers."

"I don't like flowers."

"You will someday . . ."

Joel turned off the lamp. He could almost hear Gran's voice. Odd, he thought, how vividly he remembered that day after all these years. Gran had died when he was a senior in high school, leaving the greatest void in Joel's life he had ever known, before or since. It was as if one of the main pillars of his existence had been snatched from beneath him and he'd been cruelly tossed into a large, inescapable well of loneliness.

Fortunately, he'd graduated from high school that spring, and the following fall, he'd chosen to attend a college in the East, one where there was hustle and noise and voices and laughter and shouts and games. No more Oklahoma for him, not ever.

Ingrid went into the kitchen to try to decide what frozen food she could thaw for dinner. The freezer was very well stocked, as were all the cupboards, a standard procedure in that part of the country. Often the roads were blocked for days, making trips to the store impossible. While she was mulling over her inventory, she heard Joel come up behind her. He, too, peered into the freezer, but it was obvious his mind was on other things.

"Hmmm, you smell good. Look good, too. That's quite an outfit. You look like Paree."

Ingrid couldn't help but be pleased at the compliment, but she was glad her back was to him. She wouldn't want him to think the giveaway smile on her lips and the slight tremble in her hands were caused by the husky warmth of his voice or his teasing blue eyes or the tantalizing masculine scent of him. She murmured a polite thank you and proceeded to investigate the freezer again. Unfortunately, Joel had the same idea.

He reached around her with a long arm that brushed her shoulder. "What about this Lobster Supreme?" he suggested, his breath warm on her hair.

"Sounds good to me," she agreed too readily, but his nearness was beginning to make her throat tighten. "We have all kinds of vegetables here, too, and fixings for a salad."

"Great. And what about dessert?"

She sighed tolerantly. Desserts were not her forte.

"The only thing I have are some grape Popsicles, which, my brother left here last summer."

Joel made a circle with his thumb and forefinger. "Perfect."

With a resigned shake of her head, Ingrid started hauling packages out of the freezer and handing them to Joel, who put them in the sink. He made such a big thing out of rushing from sink to freezer that she decided to relieve him of his duties.

"Look," she said, "why don't you fix drinks, and I'll do this?"

"Best suggestion I've heard all day. Where's the liquor cabinet?"

"Right here." Reaching into the lower cupboard, she brought out several bottles and set them on the counter. While she took out the glasses, Joel proceeded to read all the labels. He appeared to be in no hurry. In fact, he seemed to be dawdling. That gave Ingrid a moment to take in his attire, which, somehow, had changed his whole appearance. Far from the arrogant businessman, he now looked very much the country squire in his toffee-colored corduroys and beige open-necked shirt. Wisps of dark hair curled against the deep **V**, accentuating the inherent maleness of his body. Ingrid felt her pulse lurch with that unwelcome feeling of awareness again and hurried with the glasses, bumping into him several times . . . or was he bumping into her?

"What do you like?" he asked, all business.

"I'll have a bourbon and ginger ale." She opened the refrigerator and took a quick inventory of the soft drinks. "Uh-oh. We don't have any ginger ale. Just root beer."

There was a moment of silence. "Are you saying you want bourbon and root beer?"

Flopping an ice tray onto the sink, Ingrid looked up at her guest. He appeared to be dead serious, but she knew better.

"Water would be fine," she replied.

"Just water? Or bourbon and water?"

She sighed patiently. "You seem to forget I'm not on the witness stand."

"I'm sorry. I beg your pardon."

"That's all right."

"And you just want a glass of water?"

She inhaled deeply. "On second thought, make it a bourbon on the rocks."

His eyebrows rose. "Are you sure you can handle . . ."

"Just pour!"

This time the hint of a smile that had been playing at the corners of his mouth widened into a grin. With a final, amused lift of his brows, he began mixing the drinks.

Ingrid decided to leave him to his own devices. Going into the living room, she switched on several lights. It was a long, wide room with pale walls and soft green and ivory Oriental rugs. Picking up the colors from the floor were two huge oil paintings that were tied into the decor of the room by several fine Sheraton pieces. Blending perfectly into the backdrop of this unique setting were comfortable sofas, overstuffed chairs and plenty of tossed pillows in the same muted tones of the carpets. Despite the mixed periods of furniture, the room was boldly and successfully pulled together in exquisite harmony.

When Joel came from the kitchen with a drink in each hand, he paused in the doorway for a moment, his eyes sweeping the room with obvious approval. "I see before me the touch of a very talented artist," he remarked admiringly.

"I must admit I let my imagination go a little wild here," she said as she pulled the drapes to close out the wintery night. "Fortunately, it turned out all right."

"It's spectacular." He dipped his head in a salute. "My compliments to the designer."

"Thank you," she said as she sank into one of the deep-cushioned vanilla-white sofas. Reaching up, she took the drink Joel handed to her, very much aware of his gaze on her. Deliberately, she kept her eyes lowered, but raised them when he proposed a toast.

"Let's hope the weather clears," he said as they toasted each other. He paused a moment as though reconsidering, then shrugged, and added, "I suppose that's what I'm hoping."

Ingrid peered up at him through her fringed lashes, not sure she understood what he meant. She decided to take him at face value. "Our blizzards never last long. It'll be clear by morning."

"That'll be great," he said as he put his glass down on the table. "Before I get comfortable, I think I'd better call that idiot at Mount Traver who was supposed to meet my plane and . . ."

"That idiot," she interrupted, "is Peter Moggs, whose wife, Laura, just happens to be my best friend. He's a teacher at Mount Traver University and, incidentally, one of your most avid supporters."

"If he's so avid, why didn't he meet me?"

"Because of the weather, of course. Besides, Laura knew I was going to pick up little Gussie here and figured I'd be taking the pickup, so she asked me to do them a favor."

"And you agreed willingly."

She looked at him askance. "I won't say willingly, but I did agree."

"Despite your objections to my coming?" His expression was quizzical, as though he was trying to figure her out.

"Look," she explained, "I'm not objecting to their getting a well-known out-of-town speaker for their seminar. God knows, the university needs all the publicity it can get. But the art department has always played second fiddle to the law school. Just once, we'd like to be able to present something memorable to the school—a Gurion oil painting, for instance—that would hang in the library forever."

"I can understand your wanting something permanent—that's a very feminine desire. But how many people would benefit from this painting in the long run?"

"Everyone who enjoys exquisite works of art, that's who," she informed him coolly, "and believe me, there are a lot more of us than there are law students."

"Oh, for crying out loud," he argued, obviously

enjoying her sudden defensive attack. "Why can't you women expend your energies on redecorating the ladies' powder room or something?"

Instantly Ingrid was on her feet. "Well, thanks for the accolade. It's just like a man to come barging into completely foreign territory and . . ."

The phone rang, but Ingrid ignored it.

". . . immediately start to criticize, condemn and censure the groundwork that we have spent years laying . . ."

"Your phone's ringing."

". . . You don't understand that the very history of mankind is depicted in the intensity, the melodrama and the rich colors . . ."

"Want me to answer it?"

". . . of civilizations long ago buried beneath the ruins of ancient cities . . ." She hardly realized Joel was crossing the room to the study and absently followed him.

"Hello," he said into the receiver.

"Does anyone around here take advantage of these exhibitions when they're brought to our country from . . ."

"Laura. Glad to meet you. Joel Stires here."

". . . all over the world. Just one hundred miles from here is one of the finest museums in the world but . . ."

". . . we missed the exit ramp and decided to . . . nine in the morning, you say? That would be fine. . . . Nice talking to you, too, Laura."

When she saw Joel replacing the receiver she suddenly stopped and asked, "Who was that?"

"Laura just called to say hi." There was a maddening twinkle of amusement in his eyes.

"She never calls just to say hi."

"Well, actually, she wanted to know if you thought the culture of the community needed uplifting." His expression was absolutely deadpan.

Suddenly Ingrid realized what had happened. Pretending to be miffed, she blew her cheeks out and, exhaling a loud "Men!" she went back to the kitchen and made a great show of shoving around the pans and dishes.

Joel followed immediately and, leaning against the doorjamb with maddening nonchalance, watched her work. She slid him a slightly reproving glance. "Are you just going to stand there while I slave away unwrapping these packages?"

"If there's anything I can do . . ." he offered politely.

"As a matter of fact, there is." Drying her hands, she walked over to him and draped the towel over his arm. "Why don't you get dinner while I make a phone call?"

"Get dinner?" he repeated, incredulous.

"Sure." She gestured toward the sink with a wide arc of her arm. "There's the frozen food, and there's the microwave. Now, if you'll excuse me . . ." She started out of the room, but once again Joel seemed to be filling the doorway. This time he made no effort to move. He waited until she glanced up, then with a mischievous grin, he bent his head and kissed her lightly on the tip of her nose. "I'll say one thing, you certainly know how to delegate authority."

"Just a little something I learned in school," she replied and, ducking under his arm, escaped into the foyer. As she walked toward the study, she took a deep, stabilizing breath. There was no denying her attraction to him, nor his to her. Thank God he was leaving tomorrow, she thought. It wouldn't take much for her to get caught in his web of charm and daring, definitely not an intelligent thing to do. Yet she couldn't resist touching the tip of her nose where the warmth of his lips still lingered.

Shaking herself out of her ridiculous preoccupation with Joel Stires, Ingrid dialed her mother's number. Her seventeen-year-old brother, Kipp, answered on the first ring.

"How's Gussie?" was his greeting.

Ingrid laughed. "I'm fine, Kipp, thanks for asking. And so is Gussie. I'm just getting ready to feed her."

"Aren't you bringing her over here?" he asked, obviously disappointed.

"Tomorrow," Ingrid promised. "The roads are too bad to go out tonight." As Kipp went into his familiar diatribe about the lousy weather, Ingrid found herself listening with only half an ear. Her attention wandered quickly to the kitchen, from which sounds of a meal in progress began to emerge. Suddenly she wanted to be there, helping Joel, standing near him. Ridiculous of course, but just the same, she was glad her conversation with Kipp was a short one.

As soon as she hung up, she hurried back to the kitchen to see how her cook was doing. And to her surprise, he was doing quite well.

Giving the microwave oven a friendly pat, he beamed proudly. "It's all in here, snug as a bug. Now, what do you say we have another drink to celebrate this fete?"

"You go ahead. I'm still working on my first one."

"All right," he said, "and between sips you can make the coffee and set the table." When Ingrid shot him a wry glance, he added quickly, "That's called delegation of authority."

"Just don't carry it too far."

"Oh, no, never," he assured her, handing her two glasses. "Here, put these on the table, will you? And then you can start stacking some of these dishes in the dishwasher and cleaning up the sink and . . ." He looked around.

"And clean the oven and sweep the floor and shovel the walk," she finished.

Joel's mouth widened into a smile of approval. "You're a good woman, Ingrid."

She smiled back. "I'm glad to hear that. For a moment I thought you had me confused with a slave." Taking the glasses, she gave him a queenly toss of her head and marched into the dining room.

As soon as she was out of Joel's sight, she allowed herself a long, satisfied sigh. He was certainly different from anyone she'd known before. And, despite his apparent big-city life-style, he had made himself very much at home in her country kitchen. Unlike her, he seemed to adjust to new surroundings very well, she mused as she set the table with her nice china and even lighted a cluster of five candles in a crystal sconce.

She'd never used it before, though she'd had it for years, but tonight, for some reason, she felt like celebrating. Maybe it was Joel's cheery presence, and then again, maybe it was because she and Rob had so seldom sat down to dinner together. He'd always seemed to be rushing off somewhere, always in a hurry, traveling the fast lane. Even Ingrid had to admit that since his death she'd known peace for the first time in many years. And though she missed him terribly and was often alone, she was never lonely.

"Ready at this end," came a yell from the kitchen.

Ingrid hurried in to help. "I've been sitting there for five minutes with knife and fork in hand," she joshed. "What's holding you up?"

"Nothing. Let's go."

Joel handed her two plates, both heaped with food, then he placed his hands on her shoulders, turned her around and headed her out the door. He followed shortly with the salads, then dashed back for the melted butter. As Joel sped back and forth, Ingrid was reminded momentarily of Rob, but the image blurred when she felt Joel's firm hand on her shoulder as he pulled her chair out for her.

Ingrid had placed their seats next to each other instead of at opposite ends of the table, much to Joel's obvious delight. As soon as he sat down, he bumped her knees with his. Mumbling an apology, he scuffled around a lot and moved over a little. But when he was all through, his knees were still resting against hers. Ingrid slid him a warning glance, but he was so busy with his salad that he missed it. At least it appeared so, but she didn't make an issue of it, swinging her legs to one side. She was simply too hungry and too tired to worry about such minor infractions of etiquette.

The lobster was pink and tender, the vegetables steaming hot. A long period of silence engulfed them as they savored every morsel. Joel swore it was the best meal he'd ever eaten and proceeded to partake of everything on the table, including a dozen dinner rolls. Then sighing expansively, he leaned back in his chair.

"If my ex-wife could have cooked like this, I'd have never divorced her."

Ingrid cast him a reproachful glance. "I hesitate mentioning it, but you cooked this meal yourself. Couldn't you have done that when you were married?"

"Sure, if someone put it all on the counter and said put this in the microwave."

"You sound about as helpless as my husband. He couldn't even make a pot of coffee."

Joel nodded, understanding, then asked. "How long ago did he die?"

Ingrid noticed he didn't bother tiptoeing around her feelings, and she appreciated that. Though she'd accepted Rob's death a long time ago, it was often hard for her to speak of him in the past tense. Yet with Joel, she felt comfortable about it.

"Just a little over a year ago."

"He was awfully young for a heart attack, wasn't he?"

"Forty-four, but he'd had a serious heart murmur all his life. A year before he died, he'd had a very bad attack and was told to take it easy."

"And did he?"

"He tried to, I'll give him credit for that. He divested himself of all his gas well interests and sold his horses and most of the barn equipment. Then he paid off every debt he had and put the rest of the money aside for me."

Joel raised an eyebrow. "It sounds as if he was getting ready to die, doesn't it?"

"That's what I thought at the time," she answered quietly, absently toying with her silverware. "But he was a very restless person. When his affairs were finally all settled, he decided to become a protector of wildlife."

"That sounds serene enough."

"Right," she said. "It sounds serene enough. The only trouble was, Rob threw himself into the undertaking with his usual gusto. He made a project out of what kinds of grasses to plant and berries to grow and shelters to build, and before either of us realized it, he was right back into his same old habits." Propping her elbow on the table, she rested her chin in her hand. "I suppose I should have seen it coming and put a stop to it, but it was so typical of him to do this, that I just didn't see it."

Putting his hand over hers, Joel squeezed it gently. "You couldn't have done anything about it anyway, Ingrid. There comes a time in everyone's life when they have to take the reins and ride that last mile alone."

"You make it sound so preordained."

"Not at all, but you have to be realistic about it. If I were in his place, I'd have done the same thing—run like hell right down to the finish line. I couldn't stand to spend the rest of my life sitting around taking it easy, and from what you tell me, Rob couldn't either."

Pulling her hand out from under his, Ingrid sat back in her chair and crossed her arms. "Would it ever occur to you to think of those you left behind?"

"As a matter of fact," Joel paused thoughtfully, "I've never thought of that. Maybe that's because I don't have anyone to leave behind."

Ingrid, who had always lived within the circle of a large family, found this hard to believe. "Don't you have any relatives at all?"

"My father's still alive. I never see him, though." He raised his eyes to hers. In the flickering light they shone like bits of blue cobalt. "About three years ago I went back home to the little town in Oklahoma where I grew up, but there was nothing there anymore. I visited with my dad for one day, and he hadn't changed at all." Joel shook his head as if, to this day, he couldn't believe it. Then he lifted his eyes to Ingrid's. "Wouldn't you think a man who hadn't seen his only son in six years would be anxious to talk to him? To visit? Find out how he was doing?" He shook his head. "Not my dad, no siree. To begin with, he had a girl friend living with him, and when he wasn't ogling her, he was on the phone. I stayed exactly two hours, told him I had a business appointment and left." He threw his napkin down on the table. "I'd never go back."

"I wouldn't either," Ingrid agreed. "He probably doesn't want you anyway."

"You're right. He never did want me."

Ingrid sensed the disapproval in his voice and was surprised at this soft spot of animosity. Her brows lifted, questioning. "What do you care? He never abused you, did he?" When Joel shook his head, she went on. "He fed you and sheltered you and educated you. And if he never loved you, so what? He did the best he could."

Joel shrugged. "I suppose he did."

"Then why are you still resentful?" Ingrid pressed.

"I'm not . . ."

"Oh, yes, you are." Leaning forward, she captured his eyes with hers. "Are you afraid you might be turning out to be exactly like him?"

A swift shadow of anger crossed Joel's face, but, just as swiftly, he brought himself under control again. A man of great self-restraint, she thought, a trait that had probably been very hard for him to learn.

"How can I be just like him if I don't have a child to ignore?"

Ingrid shook her head. "That's not what I mean and you know it. Your father was so business oriented that he didn't know or care what went on around him." She leaned forward in her chair. "Do you feel you're doing the same thing?"

His answer was a quick "Of course not." Then, suddenly, he shoved his chair back from the table and stood up, indicating that the subject was closed, but Ingrid was not to be so easily dismissed. He had probed into her feelings and now it was her turn.

She remained seated. "What about your wife? Did she want children?"

Joel expelled an exasperated sigh. "Yes, your honor, she did want children. In fact, that was one of the reasons we got a divorce." He leaned down until his face was barely inches from hers. "Now is there anything else you want to know?"

Ingrid nodded firmly. "Yes." She lifted her face to his. "Do you like children?"

"I have nothing against kids." He shrugged indifferently. "I just don't have time for them, that's all."

"Not even a few minutes a day?"

Joel's brows lifted with amusement. "Am I on the witness stand?"

"Yes," she replied firmly. "Don't you have any desire at all to have a child of your own?"

"Frankly, I've never given it a great deal of thought. I travel so much, I wouldn't be able to spend much time with children anyway. Now," he said, draping his arm across her shoulders, "what do you say we forget about my paternal shortcomings and pour some coffee?"

Ingrid knew the subject was closed forever and, though she felt a little disappointed over his flippant attitude toward children, she also realized it was none of her business. "Okay," she said, "I give up." Taking cups and saucers down from the cupboard, she set them on the counter. "If you'll pour, I'll feed the dog."

Chapter Four

At the mention of the word *dog*, Gussie emerged from her makeshift bed in the corner and stood at attention in the center of the floor.

"It's a deal," Joel agreed, eyeing the dog skeptically. "But I wouldn't give her too much if I were you. She still looks like a pig . . . if you'll pardon the expression."

"That's because she's pregnant," Ingrid informed him as she scooped a half can of dog food into a bowl.

"Pregnant!" Joel gaped with disbelief. "You mean you knowingly bought a pregnant dog?"

Ingrid's disbelief matched his. "But of course. If I'm going to raise French bulldogs and she's the only one in the area, how am I going to breed her?"

Joel stroked his chin thoughtfully. "You have a point."

"It's done all the time," she assured him as she set the dish on the floor. "Now what about that coffee? Are you saving it for breakfast?"

"Coming up."

As he poured the coffee and added cream, Ingrid watched the deft movements of his hands and wondered if they would ever hold a child . . . or a woman. But of course they would. He was too blatantly male to live a monk's life, and too handsome not to be desired by every woman he met. Even Ingrid found him totally captivating, and she had barely met the man.

"Why don't we sit in the living room?" she suggested, picking up her cup and leading the way. Joel nodded wordlessly and followed close behind her, so close that she could feel his eyes on her back. Had he been studying her also?

Setting her cup on the coffee table, she sank into the protective depths of the sofa cushions, so warm and snug against the storm outside—as well as the one growing within her. Her sense of security was short-lived, however. Instead of taking the chair opposite her, Joel sat down beside her, his sleeve brushing against her arm. She started to move over, but he stretched his arm across the back of the couch and faced her, being deliberately provocative.

Instead of making an issue of his aggressiveness, she pretended to be unaware of his nearness and, forcing a casualness into her voice, asked, "Why do you have to travel so much? I thought lawyers had big offices and sat behind huge desks and took notes."

"Oh, no," he smiled. "Secretaries do that. I spend most of my time in court."

"Defending criminals?"

"No, my clients aren't criminals. They're victims of circumstance."

"But they're wealthy, aren't they?"

"Yes. What's wrong with that? Just because they're wealthy doesn't mean they're guilty. They want quality and they're willing to pay for it, and my firm just happens to be one of the top ones in the country when it comes to criminal law."

"From what I've heard," she said, leaning forward to reach her cup, "some of these famous murder trials are almost like stage productions. You have to be an actor first and a lawyer second."

He nodded grimly. "Unfortunately, that's true. Take our trial that's coming up in Cleveland next month. A wealthy industrialist named Borgas Canelli is accused of murdering his wife. Now everyone wants to get on the bandwagon. Including Mount Traver University," he added pointedly.

"What do you mean?"

"You don't think they hired me just to talk to their students, do you? They wanted the publicity."

Ingrid's brow slanted in a frown. "I don't understand."

"It's simple enough. This one's going to be a real juicy media event. Canelli is an ex-politician. He's wealthy, handsome, loquacious, the perfect star for their show. Also, he's hired a well-known law firm from New York to defend him."

"Sounds like all the ingredients for a good drama," she agreed, but she didn't add that Joel's own overpowering personality and impressive good looks could only add to the excitement.

"And Mount Traver isn't one to overlook this golden opportunity," he went on. "They're a small, private university, heavily endowed, with a very good pre-law program. But, like all universities, they need publicity. So what could be better," he said with a wave of his hand, "than to get Borgas Canelli's lawyer to speak at their seminar on the criminal personality?"

Ingrid set her cup down on the table. "But if you knew they were just using you, why did you accept?"

"For the same reason they asked me. Publicity."

"You want publicity, too?"

"Of course. This is what we call pretrial publicity. And it's invaluable. If we can get the press on our side before the trial even begins, we're halfway there."

Ingrid shook her head. "I don't think it's fair that a murder trial, or any other trial, for that matter, should be treated as entertainment. Not that I'm so naive as to think this doesn't happen every day."

She could almost see Joel being interviewed on television. He'd come across as strong, assertive and confident. And devilishly handsome. No jury with a woman on it would ever hand his client a guilty verdict. Did he know that? she wondered.

Suddenly Ingrid was aware of the warm heaviness of Joel's body as he pressed against her. She swung him a warning glance. "Your coffee's getting cold."

"That's the way I like it."

"On a night like this, I should think you'd want something warm."

"I do." His gaze never wavered.

She knew he was just teasing, just being ornery. "Then drink up," she ordered in her firm, schoolteacher's voice.

With a final, bedeviling glance down the length of her lounge suit, he sat forward, to Ingrid's relief. She didn't want him to notice the flush rising in her cheeks.

Finishing his coffee, Joel set his cup down and glanced across the room. "Why don't I build a fire in the fireplace?" he suggested idly.

"Oh, no, not that," Ingrid cut in quickly. "The chimney doesn't draw well. That's on my list of things to be looked at."

"Who would you get way out here to look at a chimney?"

"My brother or my dad. They just live five miles from here . . . which reminds me," she said, getting up. "I'd better call my mother and tell her you're here, not that she doesn't already know."

"You think Laura told her?"

"Of course. Out here it's a duty to keep your neighbors informed of what's going on."

He swung her a challenging glance. "And what *is* going on?"

"Nothing," she stated firmly. "Absolutely nothing."

To emphasize her point, she tilted her head and looked fully into his eyes. In the muted light, they were like liquid blue shadows and for a moment everything was blocked out except the magnetism of his nearness. Clearing her throat, she hurried into the study.

"Why don't you get yourself a drink?" she suggested. "I'll just be a minute."

"Good idea. Do you want one?"

"No, I don't think so. I'm going to bed pretty soon. I'm dog tired."

She didn't add that she was also worried about her body's tumultuous response to him. Even now her pulse was hammering like a drum.

Ingrid decided that if there was ever an award for tact, her mother would win it.

"Laura called and told me you'd gotten home all right. How's the dog?" Not a word about her guest.

"A real beauty, Mom, and a wonderful disposition." Then, "My guest is fine, too . . . a little restless, but he's a gentleman."

She could almost see her mother's body sag with relief. "I'm sure glad to hear that. Frankly, I was getting worried. You never know nowadays."

"Mom, don't worry. He's extremely polite. You couldn't ask for anyone nicer if you'd picked him out yourself." She didn't think it was necessary to mention that he was also the most attractive man to ever hit Ohio.

"I'm happy to hear that." Her mother sighed. "Your dad and I were getting concerned. He could have stayed over here, you know, but it doesn't look like the roads will be cleared until tomorrow."

"Stop fretting, Mom. I'm all right. In fact, I'm having

a wonderful time. It's nice to have a man around the house for a change, in case anything should go wrong."

"Yes," her mother demurred. "I suppose that's important, especially on a night like this."

They talked for several more minutes, promising to speak again the next day. Then Ingrid went back into the living room, where Joel was sitting in a chair reading a news magazine.

"Is your mother all upset about your unexpected houseguest?" he asked.

"She was at first, but I assured her you were the perfect gentleman."

Joel glanced up quickly and looked directly into her eyes. "And I am, too. I hope you realize that."

"Of course," she murmured.

"I would never take advantage of you, Ingrid."

"I know that."

"However, if you want to take advantage of me, I wouldn't object."

"That's very gracious of you, Joel."

He nodded serenely. "As I said, I'm the perfect gentleman."

His words of reassurance were also an invitation, and Ingrid realized it wouldn't take much for her to become lost in his compelling gaze. He had a way of making her feel like a very desirable woman, something her vanity found hard to resist.

"Perhaps you wouldn't mind, then, if I went to bed a little early. Maybe you'd like to watch TV?"

"I'm going to finish this first." He raised his glass. "Then maybe I'll watch the news." He got up then and, coming over to her, took both of her hands in his in a warm, intimate grip. As his blue eyes reached down into her dark brown ones, she knew she should back away from him, but she didn't . . . couldn't.

His voice was soft and wondrously low. "Seriously, Ingrid, I want you to know I appreciate your generous hospitality. Not many people are willing to share their homes with strangers, regardless of the circumstances." His grip tightened ever so slightly. "You're a good sport, Ingrid, and I want you to know if you ever need a criminal lawyer, my services are free."

His features remained absolutely unreadable. What an actor.

"Your generosity is overwhelming," she assured him, her expression as deadpan as his.

The corners of Joel's mouth tipped upward in a mildly roguish smile as, gently, he curved his hand around the back of her neck and tipped her head back. "I wonder if you know how very desirable you are," he whispered.

Ingrid tried to remain motionless, detached, not daring to allow herself to respond. But there was no way she could quell the rush of blood through her veins as she watched his mouth descend to cover hers with commanding mastery. His lips were so sensuous, so compelling, that her body, hungry after a year of abstinence, reveled in the feel of his fingers at the back of her neck, his warm breath on her face, his mouth tenderly possessing hers.

He pulled away slowly, and for a long moment looked deep into her eyes. Then, almost gruffly, he released her. "Off to bed with you before I scrap my role of gentleman and do something we will both enjoy."

Smiling, Ingrid shook her head and stepped away from him. "In that case, good night."

"Good night, Ingrid."

Though she hated to leave, Ingrid hurried to her room. She was doing the right thing; they both knew that. Yet, somehow, she felt as if she'd been watching an exciting play and had had to leave before it was over. It was maddening. It was also the correct thing to do, she reminded herself firmly.

Undressing, Ingrid slipped into a warm granny gown and creamed her face. She had a square chin and sharp features and would have looked stern but for her eyes. They were almost Indian black, round, slightly tilted at the outside and fringed with thick, dark lashes. As Ingrid rubbed the cream from her face with a tissue, she leaned into the mirror. Her skin was flushed from the tremors of excitement that tingled in every part of her body. But this was only normal, she told herself. They would dissipate as soon as Joel left. Yet, it was nice to know that her body was still responsive. It was as if something new had walked into her life.

Usually Ingrid didn't allow herself to indulge in such crazy fantasies. She'd worked too hard to get control of her life after Rob's death. But Joel Stires was different. She could allow herself a few whimsical dreams as far as he was concerned since he'd be gone in the morning and her life would continue on its even course.

In bed, she restlessly turned her head on the pillow

and tried to wish away the throbbing awareness burning within her, but the dull ache of desire was not easy to ignore, or to conquer. However, the darkness brought with it a certain peace, and Ingrid's body gradually began to relax. The snow, the wind, the sound of the branches scraping against the side of the house made her feel warm and secure. As she snuggled deeper under the blankets and her thoughts drifted out of focus, she was unaware of the soft falling of snowflakes. Big ones, that piled one upon the other all night long.

Sleepily, Ingrid opened her eyes and blinked dreamily into the grayness of early morning. Even before she was fully awake she knew that today was a very special day, as a child knows instinctively when it's his or her birthday. The tingle of excitement that had teased her the night before was still there, and though she knew she'd only see Joel for a few minutes at breakfast, she couldn't think of a more pleasant way to start the weekend. Yawning, she rolled lazily onto her side.

Suddenly a high, piercing wail slashed through the silence of the house. The smoke alarm! Ingrid sat bolt upright. A fire as far out in the country as she lived could spread to disasterous proportions before help arrived. In one swift movement, she was out of bed and racing for the door. As she yanked it open, she sniffed the air. There was no mistaking the faint but ominous smell of smoke in the hallway. Instantly every nerve in her body tensed with fear.

Fighting down a wave of terror, she ran down the hall

to awaken Joel. When she reached the foyer, she could see a thin layer of white smoke clinging to the ceiling. It wasn't alarming in its density, but she kept running just the same, her whole body taut with anxiety.

Suddenly a voice boomed from the living room. "Turn that damn thing off!"

Automatically, Ingrid's steps veered toward the voice. "What's the matter? What's going on?" she shouted hysterically over the squeal of the alarm. But an answer was not necessary. One glance at Joel crouched in front of the fireplace, poking at a burning log, said it all.

"I told you that fireplace didn't draw," she screamed. "Now look what you've done. The whole place is . . ."

"Turn it off!"

Spinning on her heel, Ingrid rushed back to the hallway. Reaching up, she slid the smoke detector off its bracket and shook the batteries out onto the floor. The sudden silence was heavenly and should have brought with it a breath of peace, but Ingrid was so furious she wasn't even aware of the stillness. Whirling, she tromped back to the living room, her face red with anger, fear, frustration, all the emotions she'd been through in the last two minutes.

She started to open her mouth to speak, but Joel beat her to it. "This damn fireplace doesn't draw!" he bellowed as he stabbed at the burning log with an iron poker.

"I told you that last night, but you wouldn't listen," she hollered back. "The flue's clogged and it hasn't worked for . . ."

"The flue is not clogged!" he snapped. "I just inspected it."

"Inspected it! Inspected it! What do you know about flues?" she demanded, furious at his audacity. Grabbing a pair of tongs, she pushed him to one side. "Now get out of my way. I'm going to get this log out of here before it smokes up the whole house."

"Oh, no, you're not." Reaching around her, he grabbed the tongs out of her hand. "You're not putting that log outside. I've been a half hour trying to get it lighted. All we have to do is get the smoke started up the chimney, and it'll keep going. Now grab that afghan over there and start fanning."

"Afghan nothing! I'm going for the fire extinguisher."

As she turned on her heel to speed out of the room, Joel grabbed her by the arm. "No, forget it. We're better off just getting the log the hell out of here. Give me those tongs and get over there near the door, and when I say open, open it!"

Normally, if anyone dared to talk to Ingrid that way, she wouldn't budge, but these weren't normal conditions. Besides, he was taking it outside, wasn't he? And it was her suggestion that they do this, wasn't it?

Hurrying to the huge sliding glass doors, she reached through the drapes and unfastened the lock and grabbed the handle, ready to yank it open. She waited pensively as Joel wrestled with the log. Finally he got it up in the tongs, but he dropped it again and, while they both stood there and watched, it rolled to the back of the fireplace and fell behind the andirons.

"Oh, no," Ingrid said, crossing over to the fireplace. "Here, give me the tongs. I'll try."

As she started to take them, he held them out of her reach. "Not on your life. You'll drop it on the rug."

"I will not," she snapped defensively, grabbing the tongs. He pushed her back. Suddenly they both froze as they heard a soft swishing sound. Turning, they stared into the fireplace where, to their utter amazement, the smoke was spiraling upward into the chimney.

"There's nothing wrong with that flue," Joel declared, a little astonished at his own revelation. "The log just wasn't back far enough." He stooped down to inspect it closer. "Someone's pulled these andirons out. They're almost eight inches from the back wall."

Ingrid's thoughts raced backward. Several months ago Laura had brought her a basket of fresh greens and had set it in the fireplace. Was it possible Laura had pulled the andirons out and Ingrid hadn't noticed?

Evidently sensing her puzzlement, Joel, to her surprise, didn't press the argument any further. Ingrid thought this was very tactful of him until she realized the reason for his silence was because he'd found another diversion—her long granny gown. It covered her completely and was heavy enough to be opaque, but still she felt undressed. Maybe that was because, by comparison, Joel seemed so fully clothed in his dark blue warm-up suit. And then, maybe it was because of the subtle humor that lurked behind his hooded eyes and the sense of breathlessness she felt.

She refrained from clutching her hand to the neck of her gown like the heroine in a silent movie. She did, however, turn away from him and start toward her bedroom. "I'd better get dressed before I catch pneumonia," she murmured.

Joel, reluctant to see her go, took a step toward her. "But what about this smoke?" he asked with a carefully placed note of concern in his voice. "Don't you want to open the doors a minute and let it out?"

"Wonderful idea," she agreed pleasantly, "and I'm sure you can handle it alone."

He turned toward the draped windows, his face a blank mask. "I don't know how to open those curtains."

"You pull the cord." He was not enticing her back into the living room, she promised herself that.

As if dazed by the sudden overwhelming project that had been thrust upon him, Joel moved cautiously toward the drapery pull. Reaching up, he gripped the wooden knob and, turning to Ingrid, lifted a puzzled brow. "This one?"

"That's the one," she stated firmly, making no effort to go to his assistance despite the fact that he fumbled around with the cord as if confused. "And don't tell me it's stuck or something," she added in her I'm-on-to-you voice.

She could see he was trying not to smile. Apparently defeated, he sighed dramatically and gave the cord a steady pull.

Acres of snow-covered woodland stretched as far as the eye could see in one of the most spectacular panoramas the wilderness could possibly produce. Even Joel stood stock-still and stared, absolutely mes-

merized at the magnitude and splendor of the countryside that had unfolded before him. It was as if nature
had placed one of her most precious gifts at their feet.
Both of them stood in silence for several awed moments.

Then a sudden gasp escaped Ingrid's throat. "Oh my
God! There must be twenty inches of snow out there! I
can barely see the tops of the scrub grass, and that
comes over my knees."

"It sure is beautiful," Joel marveled, obviously unaware of the fact that they were snowed in. Ingrid hated
to impart the bad news. He was so thrilled with the
resplendent spectacle before him that it seemed a crime
to bring him back to the travails of reality.

She watched silently as he opened the door a few
inches, making a neat slice through the great mound of
snow that had drifted against the glass panel. For
several minutes they simply stood there, their eyes still
feasting on the landscape. Then Ingrid felt the cold air
creep around her shoulders and shivered uncomforta-
bly.

"I think I'd rather have the smoke than that icy cold
air," she said, rubbing her arms.

He lifted his eyes to hers. "Do you want me to close
it?"

She nodded without answering. Her attention had
wandered to Joel's well-toned athletic physique silhou-
etted against the backdrop of white. He was so vibrant-
ly male, she thought, fighting down the pulse beat in
her throat.

With his back to her, Joel started to slide the door

shut, but he paused to scoop up a small clump of snow and toss it outside. Then he pushed the door again, but it stuck. Peering down at the floor track, he assured himself it was clear before trying again. It still didn't budge.

"This thing's stuck," he complained.

Ingrid sighed heavily. "It is not," she said, crossing toward him. "Honestly, I've never in my life seen a man as helpless as you are. Anything more intricate than opening a drape is beyond your realm." Reaching the door, she grabbed the handle and pushed. Immediately it slid into place and locked into the adjoining panel with ease.

"There," she said with finality, but she knew that even Joel could have mastered that one. She wasn't surprised, then, when she felt his arm around her shoulder.

Idly, he fingered the lace on the edge of her collar. "I sure wish I was as clever as you are." His touch was light but tantalizing.

"Oh, you are," Ingrid assured him, trying hard to fight down her inner excitement. "In fact, you're one of the cleverest men I know, on stage or off."

His thumb trailed from the ruffle of her collar to the soft flesh of her neck and jaw. "Thank you for the compliment," he whispered, kissing her hair. "Maybe we should discuss this . . . in the bedroom."

"Not on your life," she said, breaking away from him, and it wasn't easy to do with him so close, so vibrant. Sternly, she cleared her throat. "We have work to do," she informed him in her most businesslike tone.

He looked puzzled. "What kind of work? Breakfast?"

"Yes, as a matter of fact, that's an excellent suggestion. You can start by making the coffee. And if you don't know how," she said, "just bumble through it somehow while I get dressed."

"Frankly, I like what you're wearing."

"So do I, but it's just not very practical on a snowy day."

"I hate that word 'practical,'" he grumbled as they headed toward the hallway, "but I suppose you're right. In fact, I'd better get dressed myself. I can hardly show up at the seminar in this."

Ingrid cleared her throat. The time had come. "Has it occurred to you that the seminar probably has been canceled?"

He looked at her, astonished. "Why?"

"I do believe we're snowed in."

"Snowed in?"

"Yes. Same as snowbound, an old Swiss term meaning . . ."

"Snowed in? We're snowed in?" his voice rose with every word.

Ingrid could tell by the tightening of his jaw that the situation was not to his liking. The storm had created a condition over which he had no control, not the sort of thing Joel Stires would accept easily.

His first reaction was rejection. "I can't believe they'd cancel a seminar just because of a little snow. Doesn't Mount Traver have its own snow removal equipment?"

"That's not the point. The roads leading to Mount Traver are blocked. Take this one." She gestured toward the kitchen window. "It could take all day just to clear the county roads, to say nothing of my driveway, unless, of course, you feel like putting your shoulder to the shovel."

"I usually exercise in a gym."

"Don't you like fresh air?"

"Sure, but—"

"Good, then why don't you take Gussie out for a few minutes since you're dressed and I'm not?"

Joel looked down at the floor. Gussie had taken refuge in her doggy basket, the pink blanket wadded under her. Dog eyed man and vice versa. Neither one showed much exuberance over the encounter.

Ingrid realized she'd have to bargain. "I'll make a deal with you. You take the dog out and I'll put the coffee on."

He considered that for a moment. "How about you fixing the breakfast, too? If you throw that in, I'll take your pooch for a nice, long walk. Of course," he added, lifting a teasing brow, "I'll expect you to wear that gown while you cook."

"No way," she announced firmly. She was all too conscious of the tingling delight that had begun to flow through her as soon as she realized they were snowed in. But she also knew that she'd have to put a curb on her thoughts. It was one thing to let herself dream a little when she knew Joel would be leaving in a matter of hours, but if they were going to be together for the rest of the day and possibly even tomorrow, the situation could become a little more complicated than she'd bargained for.

Taking Gussie's leash down, she handed it to Joel and was just starting toward the hall when the phone rang. Retracing her steps, she answered it in the kitchen.

Peter Moggs greeted her with a cheery good morning. "I understand you have a houseguest," he began. "Just tell me one thing. What kind of a mood is he in?"

Ingrid smiled at the question. Evidently news of Joel's volatile temperament had preceded him. "I'll let you talk to him," she said, and without another word handed the phone to Joel, who was studying the intricacies of the snap on the dog's leash. "For you. It's Peter Moggs, the seminar director."

He took the phone. "Joel Stires here," he announced as Ingrid escaped down the hall to her room. If Joel was going to explode over this bit of bad news, she didn't want to hear it. Yet, instinctively, her ears strained for snatches of conversation.

"I understand the situation," she heard him say in a surprisingly calm voice. "Nevertheless I'm in a very difficult position. Not only am I imposing on my most gracious hostess, but I have a transportation problem. Seminar or not, I have to be back in New York by tomorrow evening."

Was it her imagination or did Joel sound almost content to stay over another day? But why? There was absolutely nothing for a man of his high-speed disposition to do out here in the country. Or was he expecting her to entertain him? Well, if that was the case, his plans were in for a little disarrangement. Ingrid had no intentions of getting involved with him on a personal level. Admittedly, she was as attracted to him as a bird to a tree, but she was also aware of the brevity of their association.

Determined to keep their relationship on an impersonal basis despite her vulnerability, she strode confidently into her bathing room and started the shower. She looked longingly at her luxurious bath tub, but a bath would have to wait until another day. Hurrying, she showered and dressed, pulling on jeans and a heavy cable-knit sweater, then ran a comb through her dark, silky hair, dashed on a little lipstick and hastened to the kitchen to put on the coffee.

Chapter Five

The snap of the cold brisk air combined with the sight of the bright morning sun reflecting off acres and acres of new fallen snow were unusual sensations for Joel. Drawing in several lungfuls of air, he started kicking a path toward the truck. Gussie followed in his footsteps, but since she was so hampered by the drifts, Joel unsnapped her leash. She couldn't go anywhere anyway, he reasoned, as he continued down the driveway.

Not a trace of last night's tire tracks remained, and he had to guess his way, using the swath cut through the trees to guide him. Plunging his hands into his pockets, he furrowed down to the end of the drive, then stopped and looked up and down the road. Nothing moved, not even a twig, and there was no noise, no sounds whatever. To a man who was normally in such complete control of his environment, it seemed almost unbelievable to Joel that he could be isolated by one of nature's winter whims. It made him feel a little uneasy, as if he were out of control. Joel was a man who knew that control meant power; this situation left him feeling shorn, bereft.

In the courtroom Joel was always in charge. He could control people with his rapid fire questions, his dramatic pauses, and his outbursts of objections. Or he could torment a reluctant witness, challenge the defendant, test the judge's patience and pamper the jury, all at the same time. His job was like the game that was played by the rest of corporate America. Success was everything, and winning was more important than how you played. It was almost a golden rule.

With a resigned shake of his head, Joel turned back to the house. As he retraced his footsteps, the only marks on the virgin snow, he began to think back, to think of Marilyn.

They'd met when he was still in the public defender's office and she was a court clerk, and they had gone together a year before they'd gotten married and moved into a small apartment on New York's East Side. One of their few assets was a car, and on weekends they'd driven out to the suburbs to look for "the perfect house." It became a game with them. Marilyn would invariably choose a small brick bungalow with a nice lawn and a two-car garage. But Joel always set his sights on the two-story Tudors with wide sweeping drives and trees and rock gardens. His philosophy was, why settle for less? and Marilyn's was, why wait forever? Better less than nothing at all.

They'd been married three years when Joel's big break came. Stanley Carmichael, of Carmichael and Brenhoun, the most prestigious criminal law firm in New York, had been impressed with Joel's performance in court and had offered him a job. Naturally Joel had grabbed at the chance. He'd been in the public defender's office for five years and, though he enjoyed his work, he knew his chance for advancement was nil. Besides, at that time, he had been thirty years old, and he'd felt that if he didn't grab this big opportunity with an established firm, he'd probably never have another chance.

Marilyn was just as elated as Joel, and she started house hunting in earnest. But Joel was still reluctant.

"We're not getting any younger," she'd told him. "If we're going to start a family, it'd better be soon."

Joel agreed, but still he wasn't ready. Not yet. He knew his new job would require many long hours, short trips, weekends away from home. He'd never have a child under those conditions. Marilyn would just have to wait. But she didn't. She went back to Virginia and moved in with her sister. Joel never saw her again.

When Joel reached the truck, he put his hand on the hood and paused to look at the sprawling ranch house on the rise of the hill. It was sleek and artistically beautiful, but at the same time solid and honest. Its sturdiness was hidden by its tranquil charm, not unlike Ingrid, he thought, as his gaze drifted to the kitchen windows. Warm lights glistened from within and he could see Ingrid's dark head bent over some task at the counter.

He couldn't see what she was wearing and wondered if it was the same soft velour jumpsuit she'd worn the night before. An alluring thought. It had not only accentuated the curve of her breasts and the swing of her hips but had put flecks of bright amber lights in her eyes, eyes that were quiet and sensitive and lazily seductive. Every time she raised them to his, his pulse missed a beat.

Suddenly Joel straightened. What in hell was he doing out here when the most provocative woman he'd ever met was on the other side of that door waiting to serve him breakfast?

"Come on, Gussie, hurry it up," he urged as he scrambled back to the house.

Ingrid was still trying to decide what to fix for breakfast when the outside door opened and dog and man reentered. Gussie shook herself and headed straight for her bed, but Joel made a big show of stamping his feet and brushing snow from his clothes.

"If there's one thing Gussie doesn't need," he commented as he tossed her leash on a coat hook, "it's this thing. She couldn't go anywhere if she wanted to. The snow is up to my knees."

Crossing her arms, Ingrid leaned against the doorjamb and watched while he kicked off his boots and slapped the snow from his pants. "Well, don't worry about it. There's a brand-new shovel out there, so you can start on the walk right after breakfast."

The idea had more appeal than Joel liked to admit, but he eyed her with a critical squint. "Do you mean we have to dig ourselves out?" He made it sound like an impossibility. "Hasn't Ohio ever heard of snowplows?"

"Of course they have, but they'll clear the freeways first."

His expression brightened considerably. "That could take several days, couldn't it?"

"Not at all," she hastened to inform him. "We have a very dedicated snow-removal crew. They'll work around the clock until every road is cleared, but," she added meaningfully, "they won't shovel my walk for me. So . . ."

"So we'll wait until the spring thaw?"

"So we'll wait until after breakfast."

Brushing the last trace of snow from his clothes, he walked over to her, cupped her chin in his hand and kissed her lightly on the lips. "Speaking of breakfast, I don't smell anything cooking."

"Coming up."

Turning quickly, Ingrid went back to the kitchen, Joel right behind her. Though his kiss had been light and brief, the type one bestows on a favorite aunt, it had left her lips pulsing just the same. She knew she should have protested, drawn the lines then and there, but it was such a natural gesture for Joel that to make an issue of it seemed childish and petty. Yet she realized the barrier between them dropped one notch every time he touched her. And she wasn't so naive as to think Joel wasn't aware of this also. It was probably his modus operandi, and a very effective one at that, but nothing that she couldn't handle.

With her confidence back in place, Ingrid poured the

coffee with a steady hand and offered a cup to Joel. He was standing beside her staring, almost mesmerized, out of the kitchen window. Ingrid's eyes followed his. The yellow sun of early morning sprawled across the horizon, bathing the snow-covered terrain with dazzling light. It was a familiar scene to Ingrid, but no matter how many times she saw it, she was still awed by the beauty of the unblemished pastoral countryside. For many moments they silently scanned the scene that stretched before them. Joel was so quiet that she wondered if he, too, felt the strong pull of the wilderness.

But her illusions were quickly shattered. "You're not really serious about going out in this stuff, are you?" he asked.

"Of course I am. I want to check the feeding stations." She turned to him with a smile. "And I'm counting on you to lug the grain and hay while I point the way." Moving away from the window, she started busying herself with breakfast. "You wouldn't want the wildlife to starve to death, would you?"

Crossing his arms, he leaned his back against the countertop and watched her move about the kitchen with an appreciative eye. "Of course not, but you have to realize that I grew up in southern Oklahoma where we have very little snow."

"I thought you were from New York."

An easy smile played at the corners of his mouth. "I am," he admitted. "In fact, I've lived there since I got out of law school twelve years ago, but as a city dweller,

I've been protected from the elements by efficient snow-removal equipment," he argued. "My psyche isn't geared for this stuff."

Ingrid was not impressed by his logic. "Something tells me your psyche could do with a good airing." She handed him a glass of orange juice. "And I think a gripping contest between man and nature is just what you need."

Joel's eyes flicked across her face. "That may be what I need, but it's not necessarily what I want."

Ingrid pretended not to catch the innuendo, but she could feel the thread of awareness between them tighten, drawing them closer. Hurriedly, she started beating the eggs with a fury that rivaled yesterday's storm.

By the time they sat down to breakfast, Ingrid's appetite was almost as large as Joel's. As they finished off the last of everything in sight, including the coffee, Joel leaned back in his chair and stretched leisurely. He swung his eyes to Ingrid, a half smile hovering at the corners of his mouth.

"You were kidding about going outside, weren't you?"

"Not at all." Pushing her chair back, she started clearing the table. "I'll just stack these while you change into warmer clothes." She looked down at his dark blue warm-up suit. "If you have any wool socks, you'd better wear them."

"Oh, hell," he said, snapping his fingers. "Would you believe I only have one pair of very thin hose with me?"

"No, I would not, so hurry up. We want to be back inside before it starts snowing again."

"Oh, God, not that," he grumbled as he went down the hall to his room.

Ingrid couldn't help but smile as she watched him disappear. In spite of his grousing, she knew he was anxious to go outside. The telltale signs of restlessness were beginning to show, and if there was one subject she knew a lot about, it was impatience. In one way at least, she thought, Joel was like Rob—always in the fast lane.

Ingrid got into her boots and jacket and was just pulling her red cap over her hair when Joel came down the hallway toward her. He was wearing jeans snugly tucked into tight-fitting boots, a heavy jacket, gloves and a navy cap perched rakishly over his forehead.

She stood back, eyeing his tall figure with obvious approval. "Well, I must say, for someone who professes to being a city dweller, you certainly know how to dress for a cold day in the wilderness."

"My talents are boundless."

"So I see."

In the muted light of the snow room, his eyes were like bright circles of light, warm and glowing. For a moment feelings Ingrid had buried long ago began to come into focus. Then, suddenly, something clicked in her mind as a shiver of vivid recollection came to the surface. Shaking herself inwardly, she turned away from him, determined to get her resolutions back in order before she found herself with another round of painful memories to fight.

As she started for the door, Joel put his hand at the small of her back and, together, they stepped out into the glistening world of white. The weather was cold, clear and cloudless. Almost instinctively, both of them tipped their chins heavenward and took several deep, lung-filling drafts of crisp, sharp air.

"Mmmm, isn't that marvelous?" Ingrid murmured as she started toward the garage.

"I have to admit it's pretty good stuff," Joel agreed. "I'm so used to the grime of the industrial revolution that I forget there are places like this."

"Wait until we get to the woods. It's like fairyland."

"Woods?" he repeated skeptically. "Are you telling me we're going to tramp through woods where the snow is so deep that you have to be a gazelle to get anywhere?"

"It's not that bad if you keep to the ridges," she assured him. "Here, help me with this."

Together they raised the door to the garage. Inside, one wall had bales of hay stacked from floor to ceiling. Lined up against the back wall were several large metal drums. While Joel removed the lids, Ingrid took down two deep buckets from an overhead shelf and started filling them with grain and bird seed. She handed a bucket to Joel. He reached for both of them, but she held one back.

"You'll need one hand free to push branches out of your way," she advised. "Besides, the first trip is always the hardest. Just making a path takes a lot of energy, but once we've done that, we can go back and forth without any problem."

"Think of that."

"Ready?" she asked brightly.

"I suppose."

Ingrid smiled up at him. "Your enthusiasm is overwhelming."

"I was hoping you'd notice."

As they started out of the garage, Joel paused to look at the truck, parked at the end of the drive and almost completely covered with snow. "Tell me something," he said. "As long as the garage here was empty, why didn't you put the truck in it last night?"

"Oh, I don't keep the truck in the garage. I keep it in the barn with my car."

Joel looked across the landscape to a building about two hundred yards from the house. "Is that the barn way over there?" he asked, puzzled.

"Yes, that's it."

Joel simply stood there, looking from the barn where the car and truck were kept to the garage where the hay and grain were stored. Finally he just shook his head. His only comment was, "No comment." Then with more eagerness than he dared to admit, he fell into step behind his very attractive hostess.

Ingrid knew the paths well and by keeping to the ridges, she avoided most of the deep snow. Occasionally Joel sank into a drift that was well over his knees, and on these occasions, he made a big issue of the perils of the trip, the dangers of hiking in winter, the risks of getting lost and even the hazards of being attacked by deer. But Ingrid plodded on, unmindful of his complaining. She knew it was just a surface thing. Joel was the type who would dispute anything just for the sake of airing his vocal chords.

After crossing a small, open field, they entered the woodsy area. Here the snow was not as deep and the walking was much easier. They stopped a minute to rest. Ingrid looked all around her as if to assure herself that nothing had changed since the last time she had been there. This was her own private corner of the world, and she felt very protective of it.

"Did your husband plant these trees?" Joel asked suddenly.

"Yes, some of them. He had quite a forestry program underway." Setting her bucket down, she stretched her arm for a moment. "He was dedicated to improving the wildlife habitat, and planted hundreds of trees like these pines here and those crabapples and plums. There's even a cranberry copse on the other side of this hill."

"Sounds like a very enterprising undertaking."

"It was, but wildlife preservation became an obsession with him. After he got the trees in, he planted a hundred acres of food patch seed and as soon as that started to grow, he got into nesting structures for ducks and Canadian geese." Sighing heavily, Ingrid picked up her bucket and started walking again.

"Did he put up these bird feeders, too?"

Ingrid turned to Joel with a sudden smile. "No, I did. It gave me an excuse to be near him and, oh, just to walk in the woods and commune with nature once in a while."

"Sounds as if you felt a little left out."

They ducked under a low branch. "Yes, I suppose I did a little, but at the time I thought I was doing the right thing for him." She paused for a moment. "But now, thinking back, I wonder if Rob thought I was just trying to get him out from under my feet."

Joel put a reassuring hand on her shoulder. "I think you're being a little hard on yourself. You stuck with him to the end, Ingrid, and that's all any earthling can do. Remember, you're not superwoman. You're just a human being like the rest of us. You make mistakes, you fall down, you get hurt and then you get up and do the same thing all over again." He gave her shoulder a squeeze. "Welcome to the club."

"You make me feel so inept."

"I believe the word is 'normal.'"

Glancing up at him, Ingrid smiled a thank you. But for a long moment her gaze remained fixed on the rugged planes of his face. She was beginning to realize that beneath that crusty exterior was a very understanding and very compassionate man who had undoubtedly had his share of setbacks, too. Welcome to the club, he'd said. Welcome; what a lovely word.

Suddenly Ingrid realized she was staring and, swinging around, she stepped over a fallen tree and started walking again. Joel followed, silent at first, but gradually his grumblings of discontent were revived and continued until they finally reached a small clearing where deer tracks and the footprints of smaller animals were everywhere.

"Why don't I fill the feeders while you tramp down the snow?" she suggested.

"Tramp down the snow? Why?"

"Because I'm going to throw some of this seed out for the smaller animals, and I don't want it sinking out of sight into a deep drift."

"What kinds of smaller animals?"

"Squirrels, for one."

Joel stood feet apart, hands on hips, and looked all around him. "Why can't the squirrels simply climb up the tree, go out on the branch, shinny down the bird-feeder wire, then crawl . . ."

"Just start tramping, will you?" Ingrid sighed, exasperated.

"Okay, okay, but I still say it's unnecessary labor."

"But since it's so cheap, we might as well use it, right?"

Joel's mouth flattened into a straight line. "Wait until my union hears about this," he teased as he began to kick the snow around unenthusiastically.

When he was finished, Ingrid spread the rest of the grain on the ground. Then, sighing with satisfaction, she looked around her. "Now all we need is a couple of bales of hay and maybe a new salt block."

"Oh, no," Joel said, collapsing against a tree. "What about our coffee break? Our fifteen minutes at the water cooler? The company's morning exercise program?" he asked. "No. Forget that," he added hastily. Pulling himself away from the tree, he stood beside her, insolently close. "I'll settle for an office conference, though."

Ingrid grinned good-naturedly. "At the moment I can't think of anything to confer about, but maybe I

will before we're through. We still have several more
trips to make before noon."

"Noon? Does that mean we're going to stop for
lunch or is this just a cruel joke?"

"No joke. We're not only stopping for lunch, but
you're cooking it."

"That figures," he said and, putting his arm around
her shoulders, started walking her back toward the
house. "I just hope my energy lasts until then."

"I wouldn't worry about it."

As they plodded through the snow side by side, their
hips kept bumping together, more often than necessary, she noted. But she didn't care. It was a beautiful
day and she was with the most exciting man she'd ever
met. What fool of a woman would throw that away just
because a shadow hung over tomorrow?

When they got back to the garage, Ingrid produced
two large canvas bags with webbed loops on each end.
She put a full bale of hay into one and a half bale into
the other, then cut the baling twine and slid her arms
through the loops. Then she hefted the smaller bag
onto her shoulders like a knapsack. Joel followed suit,
but not without protest. He groused all the way back to
the woods.

"Even mountain climbers have it easier than this."

"But think how fortunate we are that there's almost
no wind," she rationalized.

"Just walking through this stuff is enough to kill
anyone. I hope you have industrial insurance just in
case . . ."

". . . and the sun will be in our faces most of the way. We might even get a tan."

"I can see myself explaining this to my chiropractor: 'You see, doc, I was going up a hill with this gigantic block of hay on my back and—'"

"There! Hear the birds?" she asked brightly. "They're starting to rustle out of the bushes and look for food."

"As long as they're out looking, why don't we just leave the stuff here and let them come and get it? If they're expecting room service . . ."

"Low branch. Watch your head," Ingrid cautioned.

But her warning came too late. Joel was yanked to a stop with a sudden jerk as a low bough caught in the corner of his hay pack. Instead of doing anything to free himself, he just stood there, arms hanging limply at his sides, lips pressed in a flat line of resignation.

Ingrid hurried to his assistance. "My God, I've never seen anyone as helpless as you in my entire life," she remonstrated as she broke off the tip of the branch and tossed it aside. "A two-year-old child could have worked himself out of this one."

"A two-year-old child would have been too short to have gotten involved with the damn tree in the first place," he argued. "Obviously, this is an adult problem."

"Stop complaining," she retorted, "and be glad you studied law instead of forestry. Now follow me."

Just as she swung away from him, Joel grabbed her by the shoulder and, pushing her cap down over her eyes, gave her a sound pat on the derriere. "Go ahead, sarge, I'm right behind you."

"I'm well aware of that fact," she informed him and, shoving her cap back, she started down a path, fully aware of Joel's steady gaze boring into her back—and her own tempestuous response to it.

Ingrid could hear Joel bumbling along behind her. He was a large man and with the addition of a bale of hay on his back, there wasn't a bush or shrub he didn't knock into. "If Carmichael could see me now, he'd demote me," he continued to grumble.

"Who's Carmichael?" she asked over her shoulder. "Your boss?"

"More or less. Actually, he's the senior member of our firm and one of the best criminal lawyers in the country. Surely you've heard of him? Stanley Carmichael? The smoothest tongue in the east?"

Ingrid shook her head. "I'm afraid not. Crime doesn't happen to be one of my favorite subjects. I always skip that part of the news and go on to the arts section."

"There's nothing like keeping your head in the sand."

Ingrid cast him a censorious glance. "I'm sorry, but I just can't get enthusiastic over a bunch of well-educated adults making a stage out of a courtroom for the benefit of the news media."

"We don't do it for the news media," he informed her curtly. "It just so happens that a good criminal trial is more exciting than a TV show. The viewers and readers follow it because it's real and they feel a part of it."

They reached the clearing they'd made earlier, and Ingrid lowered her pack to the ground. "And what about you? As the star of the show, do you feel a part of it, too?"

"I'm not the star of the show," he reminded her patiently. "The entire justice system is the star." He dropped his pack to the ground with a loud thump. "You seem to forget that the purpose of the 'show,' as you call it, is to decide a person's life."

"I haven't forgotten that," she said quietly. "I was just wondering if you ever did."

A slight shadow crossed Joel's face, but he masked it quickly by assuming the same expression of inscrutability he'd worn when she'd first met him at the airport. Despite their differences of opinion, she had to admit he had tremendous emotional control. No wonder he was so successful in the courtroom.

As if to prove her point, Joel gave her a small but irresistible smile. "The only satisfaction I get out of any criminal trial is knowing I've won the battle and that I'll be paid handsomely for it."

Ingrid shook her head. "I don't believe that," she said as, bending over, she pulled a section of hay from her pack and started spreading it across the ground. "From what I've observed, I'd say the money is less important to you than knowing you've outperformed your opponent. I think you're a very competitive person."

"You're no slouch in that department yourself," he declared as he tossed a double section of hay into the thicket.

Ingrid paused for a moment. "Yes, I suppose you're right. I'm a rotten loser."

"Nothing wrong with that. The ones who hate to lose seldom do." Dumping the rest of the hay from his pack onto the ground in a big pile, he straightened, finished with the job.

Ingrid scowled critically. "You're supposed to spread that around a little."

"Oh? No problem."

With three well-aimed kicks, he sent the pile of hay flying through the air in all directions. Some of it landed on the tops of shrubs, some of it caught in tree branches and some of it floated down onto Ingrid's head and shoulders.

She simply stood there, feet planted firmly in the snow, eyes shut, mouth tightly closed. Joel went to her and clumsily attempted to brush off her jacket, concentrating his efforts on the soft curve of her breasts.

"I flunked wildlife," he explained, "but I was quite good at touch football."

"So it seems." Firmly, she removed his hands from her body. "I'll do my own brushing, thank you."

"I was only trying to be of some assistance." He put a hand on the top of her head and turned her face to his. "Sure you don't need my help?"

His voice held a disturbing note of suggestiveness that made Ingrid's heart turn over in response. Fighting down the surge of excitement, she murmured, "Quite sure" and, moving away from him, she busied herself with rolling up her empty sack. There was no denying her response to him, but at the same time, she was mindful of the vast differences between them. Where she was cautious and guarded, Joel was reckless and inquisitive; it was quite a strain on a new relationship, this up and down, up and down like a seesaw.

Suddenly Joel smiled, a quick, engaging smile that immediately dismissed her uncertainties. "What do you say we break for lunch? I'll buy."

"It's a deal," she replied. Instantly all apprehensions were discarded as once again she took his arm and they made their way through the snow to the house.

Chapter Six

As they tromped up the walk and into the snow room, Ingrid looked behind her. "Oh, we forgot to shovel the walk."

Quickly, Joel hustled her inside and slammed the door with a firm thwack. "Plenty of time for that tomorrow. Right now our bodies need food and rest."

"In that case," Ingrid suggested, as she pulled off her hat and unzipped her jacket, "why don't you take a nap this afternoon while I grade some advertising posters my students handed in on Friday?" Sitting down on the narrow bench, she began tugging off her boots.

Joel sat down beside her. "No, as long as you're so hell-bent on working, I'll do the same. Unfortunately, I'm never without a briefcase full of notes to correlate."

Spreading his knees wide to remove his boots, he

leaned heavily against her. Ingrid moved over a little but, predictably, so did he.

She faced him squarely. "You take up more room than any man I've ever known."

Clamping a hand over her knee, he dug his fingers into her flesh. "Did anyone ever tell you that you suffer from territorial possessiveness?"

"Did anyone ever tell you your legs sprawl all over the place?"

"Yes, my ballet teacher . . ."

Before Ingrid could respond, they were interrupted by the sudden ring of the phone. As Ingrid went into the kitchen to answer it, she could feel Joel's eyes following her, concentrating on the sway of her hips. Suddenly she felt a sensuous tightening deep within her. It was a strange sensation, new and wonderful.

Laura Mogg's voice, as quick and breathless as usual, came over the wire. "I just called to see how you and your guest were surviving over there. God, honey, I'm sorry about this. When I asked you to pick up Joel Stires, I had no idea you'd be snowed in with him for two days. I suppose you're going out of your mind trying to entertain him."

"No, not at all," Ingrid assured her quickly. "In fact, we're managing quite well. We've been outside most of the morning filling the feeding stations."

"Hmmm," Laura mused. "Somehow he didn't come across as the wildlife type."

"He isn't, but he's learning." Ingrid wished Laura would change the subject. She was sure Joel could hear every word. "Have you heard any weather reports?" she asked suddenly.

"They're not expecting any more snow, and the freeways will be cleared by two o'clock," Laura reported dutifully.

"We should be dug out by this evening, then."

"Let's hope so, though I must say you don't sound too upset about the situation," Laura teased. "Tell me, is he as pleasant as he sounds on the phone?"

Ingrid tried cupping her hand over the mouthpiece. "I don't know, Laura, I've never heard him on the phone."

"Is he as handsome as his pictures?" she pressed.

Ingrid glanced at Joel, who was moving about the kitchen from cupboard to cupboard, looking for who-knew-what. Dressed as he was in a bulky sweater, his shoulders looked positively enormous. He was a very impressive male specimen, no doubt about that. Despite his city living, there wasn't an ounce of fat on him, just hard, sinewy muscle and . . .

"Ingrid? Are you there?" came Laura's voice.

"Yes, oh yes," she said, gathering her wandering wits back to the last question.

"I said, is he as handsome as his pictures?" Laura repeated.

"I don't believe I've ever seen one," she answered guardedly.

"How come? There's one on the bulletin board in the teachers' lounge. You mean you missed it? Honestly, Ingrid, you have to get your head out of the sand once in a while."

"I've been told that once today already," she commented dryly.

"You have?" Laura paused for a moment. "Well, all I can say is, things must be either very feisty at your house or very cozy. Too bad I can't take a dogsled over there and see what's going on. After all, I do feel responsible. Besides," she lowered her voice, "I don't want to miss anything, you know."

"I know . . ."

They talked several more minutes while Ingrid watched Joel remove a can of soup from the shelf and look around for a can opener. She knew this would be followed by an intense search for a pan, bowls, and spoons, so she rang off. Taking the can out of his hand, she turned him toward the living room and gave him a gentle shove.

"Why don't you take a stab at building another fire in the fireplace? It's chilly in here."

"Don't you have a sweater?"

"Yes. I'll get it in a minute."

"I'll get it for you. Where is it? In your room?"

She paused for a moment, then nodded. "Mmmm, I think it's over the back of the chair near the door." As he started down the hall, she called after him, "Navy blue with white buttons."

"Right."

With a little shiver, Ingrid turned back to opening the soup when it dawned on her that Joel had done a pretty good job of putting a lot of distance between himself and the cooking. Not that she cared. He was hardly kitchen material.

Suddenly Joel let out a shriek of absolute joy. "Oh, my God! Look at this bathroom!"

"Oh, no!" Ingrid cried, clapping a hand to her forehead. He'd blundered into her bathroom, her beautiful bathroom. Dropping the soup can onto the counter, she flew out of the kitchen and across the foyer. "Damn it anyway," she grumbled, "I should have known better than to send you to look for anything. You couldn't find your socks if you were wearing them. I've never known a man as pathetically disorganized . . ." She strode into her room and, as she suspected, her sweater was right there on the chair. "This is what you're looking for," she informed him curtly and picking it up, trounced into the bathroom.

Joel stood in the middle of the floor, his eyes wide with disbelief. "I've never seen anything like it," he said slowly as he turned a complete circle. His eyes absorbed everything—the white carpeting, the ruffled skirt of the dressing table, the tiled shower stall, and, lastly, the huge, round, sunken tub. He drifted over to it as if in a dream and stood looking down into the shiny blue porcelain bowl. A long sigh of awe escaped him.

"It must be seven feet in diameter," he marveled.

"Yes. Now about lunch . . ." Taking him by the arm, she tried to guide him toward the door.

"And the view!" With a wave of his arm he gestured toward the glass panels, where the rolling white hills of the countryside were revealed gleaming like jewels in the sun. Something told her it wasn't going to be easy to get him out of there.

"The soup's almost ready," she prodded. "All we have to do is set the table."

"And what's this?" he asked, picking up a small white terry-cloth roll and turning it over in his hands. "It's a pillow! What do you think of that!" He peered into the tub again. "But I can see where it'd come in handy. The bowl's so shallow and with those sloping sides you could stretch out and take a nap in it if you wanted to."

"All right!" Ingrid shouted, throwing up her hands. "This has gone far enough!" She stood directly in front of him, her eyes glaring belligerently. "Let's get something straight right now. You are not taking a bath in my tub."

"Why in hell not?" he asked.

"Because you have your own tub on the other side of the house, that's why."

"I can't use that. It's small and narrow and I'm all scrunched up in it."

"It is a standard-size tub."

"And there isn't a single plant in there, not even a hung one."

"Ivy won't grow there. It's too dark."

"And that's another thing. It's dark and gloomy in there."

"Oh, don't complain," she said, pushing him out of the room. With much shoving and hauling, she finally got him through the bedroom and into the hall. She realized he was enjoying her ministrations immensely, but she couldn't worry about that now. At least he was moving, slowly and reluctantly, but moving. She couldn't decide if he was allowing her to escort him out of the room because he was a gentleman or because he was plotting some other means of access to her bathing room, stubborn man that he was. But she had no intentions of sharing that one niche that had been hers alone ever since the house was built. Not even Rob had ever set foot in her glorious tub.

Though Joel continued with his complaining, Ingrid knew it was more out of habit than discontent. She decided to try taking his mind off the subject by plying him with food, and heated up two cans of soup, made a mound of sandwiches and even found a box of cupcakes in the back of the freezer. He ate like a harvester, but between mouthfuls he still managed to get out a few more grievances.

"I can't imagine a perfect hostess like you denying her houseguest."

"Have another sandwich?"

He took two. "An hour ago I would have said you were the most unselfish, considerate person."

"A lot can happen in an hour. Now why don't you finish up this potato salad?"

He emptied the remainder of the carton onto his plate. "It just goes to show you."

"I found a package of cupcakes in the freezer."

"Chocolate?"

"White."

"That'll do." He thought a minute. "Now where was I?"

"We were discussing dessert."

"Oh, that's right. Any more grape Popsicles?"

"Yes, but I'm saving them for a special occasion. Besides, they'll give you chills."

"I already have chills," he argued, "and I think I should build a huge fire in the fireplace." He started rubbing his arms. "I have to do something to get warmed up."

"Oh, God," Ingrid said, closing her eyes. "Don't you ever let up?"

Joel tapped her arm with the back of his hand. "You know, Ingrid, you have a habit of underestimating the needs of your guests. You really should watch that."

She opened her eyes just in time to catch the teasing grin that tipped the corners of his mouth. Her fingers ached to reach out and touch him, but she knew better than to offer him any encouragement. His streak of impulsiveness was a lot quicker than her streak of propriety.

Suddenly pushing her chair back, she got to her feet and gestured toward the table. "You'd better get started on these dishes," she advised. "There are quite a few of them."

Predictably, Joel gasped with disbelief. "I'm being exploited!"

"That's right," Ingrid agreed with a bright smile. "And about time, too."

Turning away from him, she had started to clear the dishes when two strong arms came from behind and locked across her chest. She knew she should protest, but the feel of his breath on her cheek, the firmness of his body pressing against hers, held her still. Ingrid had to struggle to keep her erratically beating heart under control, but it was as if some invisible force kept dissolving her resistance and leaving in its place the soft throb of desire.

"You smell delicious," Joel whispered into her hair. Then, tightening his grip, he added, "Feel good, too."

Slowly, he turned her toward him and, placing his hands on either side of her head, tipped her chin up to his. For a long, quivering moment he looked into the depths of her eyes. Then, lowering his head, he took her lips in an urgent, burning kiss that sent hot spirals of ecstasy through every muscle in her body. As Ingrid's blood raced crazily through her veins, everything was blocked from her mind. The only thing she was conscious of was the magnetic pull of his masculinity and her own hungry desire to possess all of him. She yearned to wrap her arms around him, draw him closer, slide her hands over his muscled frame, squeeze him to her . . . but this was not possible.

She knew it was fear that steadied her wavering impulses. To Ingrid, there was no such thing as a brief love affair. There was only forever. If she gave herself to Joel, she would be laying herself wide open to heartbreak and despair, while he would bounce back into his legal world unscathed.

Reluctantly, she stepped back out of his arms. Her foolish heart was still hammering in her chest, but she took a deep breath and casually adjusted her sweater. Beneath the facade, however, her emotions were still swirling like snowflakes in the wind.

Gently, Joel touched her cheek with the back of his

hand. "We've come a long way in a short while," he murmured.

"Yes, I know," she answered, her voice deceptively calm. Then, with great effort, she managed to get her mask of indifference firmly in place. She raised her eyes to his. "And I think it's time we came to an understanding."

She could almost feel his body tense, like that of an animal who had heard a strange sound and stood waiting in the tall grass, every muscle taut.

"I realize," she went on, "that we've been thrown into a rather bizarre situation over which neither of us has any control. But I do think, and I'm sure you'll agree with me, that we owe it to ourselves to behave as properly as possible." Straightening her sweater again, she waited for Joel's words of approval. However, instead of agreeing quickly, as she'd expected, he had the audacity to pause and think it over, as if he were the judge as well as the jury. "Just so there's no misunderstanding," she added quickly, "you don't have veto power over my suggestions."

"I understand that," he conceded, his eyes sparkling with amusement, "but what about my decisions?"

"You don't have any. I'm making them for you."

"That's tyranny," he declared, "and it'll never work." Gently, he knuckled his hand against her cheek. "And if you don't hurry up with your homework, I just might be tempted to prove it."

"You'll do no such thing. But you're right, we'd both better get to work."

Ingrid hurried out of the dining room, nervous and

strangely excited. Despite all his bluster, she knew Joel would never force himself on her. Deep inside, he had a finely tuned sense of justice. Then why, she asked herself, was she making such a fuss over maintaining their respectable distances? Was she trying to convince Joel—or herself?

Giving herself an inward shake, Ingrid went into the living room and cleared off the long library table so that she could spread out her students' exam papers. Easing down into one of the leather chairs, she put the unread stack of papers to her left, the ones she was reading in front of her, and the ones that had already been graded to her right. This was the most efficient way she knew and, as long as the papers stayed in neat piles, her task was comparatively easy. Soon she was lost in her work and only faintly did the sounds of Joel's kitchen work drift past her ears.

After spending the better part of thirty minutes reminding himself of the virtues of maid service, Joel finally placed the last glass into the dishwasher and pressed the start button. Then, wandering toward the living room, he paused for a moment in the doorway, watching Ingrid work. Though her back was almost fully turned to him, he could see her red pen dip down, make a quick efficient note and lift up again. There was almost a stern conformity in her concentration and a definite air of impatience with anything that might interrupt her work. Even a strand of hair falling across her face was quickly brushed back and tucked into place. Joel could see right away that Ingrid was a person who did not believe that work and play ever mixed. What a pity. Pity? Hell, what a waste!

Pasting his famous jury smile into place, Joel went over to the table. He was just leaning over Ingrid's chair when she looked up.

"All finished in the kitchen? Very good. You get a star." She went back to her papers.

Joel put one hand on the back of her chair and the other on the table. Noisily, he cleared his throat. "What are these? Test papers?"

"Yes, art history." She looked at him as if seeing him for the first time. "Didn't you say you had some paperwork to do?"

"Oh, yeah, sure, there's always something."

"Then why don't you get started? This is a wonderful time of day to work."

"Mmm." Joel could have thought of better ways to spend the afternoon, but he knew he was beaten before he started. So, with a resigned sigh, he left Ingrid to her work and, going to his bedroom, rooted through his suitcase until he came up with his airplane work, then returned to the living room lugging his bulging briefcase. His eyes immediately rested on Ingrid's bent head. Her shiny black hair reflected the amber tones of the fire and framed her face with a luminous softness that held him captive. She was a typical brunette, and a beautiful one, with her slender neck and high cheekbones and a wide brow that gave her face strength and determination. And yet, there was an undeniable softness about her, a vulnerability that Joel found absolutely fascinating. And there was something else, too, something he couldn't exactly define, but it filled him with an inner excitement he'd never experienced before.

Joel realized that, as a teacher, Ingrid had papers to grade and tests to prepare and that weekends were probably the only time she had for such mundane chores. Nevertheless, he couldn't help but feel that under the circumstances the least she could do was set her work aside for a while and spend a little more time with him. After all, he was only going to be here a few days. Why should she spend their precious hours together doing homework?

Actually, he knew the answer to his own question; it was an age-old problem. Ingrid's apparent preoccupation with her papers was really just a cover-up for her deeper feelings. Like all women, she wanted to feel that she was the hunted, not the hunter. But Joel didn't mind that. He was a pretty good sportsman himself, especially when the quarry had a body as young and seductive as Ingrid's. In spite of the bulky clothes she was wearing, he was fully aware of the uptilted breasts, the well-rounded hips, the shapely thighs. There was no denying it; she was sexy as hell. She was also grading papers. She was also pointedly ignoring him.

Carefully, Joel set his briefcase on the table and slowly, so as not to make any noise, he unsnapped the latch, muting the clicking sound with his thumb. Then, reaching inside with one large hand, he scooped all of the papers out onto the table, shook the case to make sure it was empty, then gently lowered it to the floor. Some of the papers were legal-size, some letter-size, but most of them were an assortment of hasty notes that he'd made on any available piece of scrap paper and stuffed into the briefcase for future indexing.

As he started to put them into piles, he realized he'd have to subdivide them again into smaller piles. By mistake, a small slip fluttered onto Ingrid's papers. Hastily, he retrieved it. "Pardon me," he murmured. He reached over to reclaim a wayward slip of yellow paper that had fallen on Ingrid's head, of all places. "Oh, excuse me." When he withdrew his hand, his elbow grazed the top of a pile, scattering quite a few notes on the table as well as on the floor. He promptly bent over to scoop them up, but when he straightened again, his broad shoulder jarred the table, causing Ingrid's neat red pen to skid across a page in a jagged line.

She closed her eyes and took a deep breath. Then, putting her pen down, she folded her hands in front of her and faced him with a long steady gaze. "Why don't you put this stuff away until you can find an empty gym to work in?" she suggested.

"I'll be organized in a minute," he assured her. "You just go ahead. Do you have to have those graded by Monday?"

Doggedly, she picked up her pen. "No, Tuesday. I don't have any classes on Monday."

"Oh?" His piles kept fusing together, so he spread them farther apart. "Then what do you do all day Monday?"

"From the looks of things, I'll be grading papers. These papers," she added dryly.

Joel was quick to detect the note of censure in her voice, but he didn't let it worry him. He knew that, even though she was in the habit of protesting everything, she wasn't really as dissatisfied as she appeared to be. Underneath her scornful frown, she had a marvelous sense of humor that he found as exciting as it was challenging. In fact, everything about Ingrid Christian had that effect on him. He couldn't help but wonder if she brought the same stimulation to her lovemaking.

Ingrid stood up and straightened her three piles of papers. "I'll tell you what I'll do," she announced. "I'll let you have the table, and I'll finish these on the couch." Without waiting for his answer she snapped her papers into a neat pile and went over to the sofa.

Joel, with no immediate excuse for not working, began the boring task of sorting and resorting, but his gaze kept wandering to where Ingrid was sitting, her head bent over her work. In one sense he felt as if he'd known her forever, and in another, he wondered if he knew her at all. Despite her blustery temper, she was a very private person, only giving tiny pieces of herself at a time. Yet he knew that under that facade of agitation, a sensuous flame glowed steadily. How steadily, he didn't know, but maybe, if he played his cards right, he could test it and see. Maybe, just maybe, he could stoke it into an inferno.

They sat for almost an hour in total silence. Even Joel managed to get some work done, but every moment he sat there he became more and more conscious of Ingrid's well-shaped, neatly composed body that, even across the room, seemed to be throbbing a vibrant message. The longer he watched her, the more he wanted to reach out and touch her, take her in his arms, fold her into his body. Suddenly she shivered. Suddenly he decided he'd worked long enough.

He got up and, after sauntering over to the couch, he dropped down beside Ingrid. "Almost finished?" he asked hopefully.

"Just about," she murmured, sliding him an oblique glance. "Why?"

He stretched his arm around her shoulders and moved a little closer. "I thought maybe we could do something together."

Turning, Ingrid faced him directly. She blinked, deliberately feigning innocence. "Are you suggesting we play a game or something? I have Trivial Pursuit, Scrabble, and Monopoly."

"They all sound wonderful," he murmured as his fingers trailed down the side of her cheek. Her skin was soft and delicate, her lips full and inviting. She raised her eyes to his and was about to speak when he covered her mouth in a warm, intimate kiss that sent an unexpected shudder throughout his whole body. Enfolding her deeper into his embrace, he could feel her response, as vibrant as his and as filled with yearning. And then her arms circled his neck and she returned the kiss with an intensity he hadn't dared hope for.

Holding her gently, as if she were a fragile bough bending in the wind, he massaged her lips, coaxed them apart and then, entwining his tongue with hers, explored the inner recesses of her mouth. Willingly, she melted into his arms, her body pulsing with the same heightened awareness he, too, was feeling.

Then, as though suddenly aware of the intensity of her reactions, she turned her head to one side and pulled out of his embrace. Joel, stunned at his own shuddering response, kissed her tenderly on the tip of her nose and nestled her silky head into his shoulder.

"Very nice," he whispered into her hair. "Much better than Monopoly."

Ingrid sighed deeply. "Something tells me I'd better get that game set up right away."

"To hell with the game. Let's just stay here like this for the rest of the day."

Tilting her head back, she looked up at him. "We both know this can only lead to a dead end."

"Well, so what?" He shrugged. "It seems to me that when two people are as physically attracted to each other as we are . . ."

"And what makes you think that?" she asked, her eyes widening.

"I can feel the vibes."

"Oh, is that right?" she mused. Leaning away from him, she eyed him skeptically. "And how did you arrive at this outlandish conclusion?"

"Simple. When I'm with you I realize I am as irresistible as I've always thought I was."

Ingrid burst out laughing. "God, you're modest, Joel."

"It goes with the job." He grinned and started to pull her closer, but Ingrid suddenly rose.

"Why don't you build up the fire?" she suggested

brightly, "and I'll go and look for a game of some kind."

Without waiting for his reply, she stepped back and almost tripped over Gussie, who had curled up beside the couch. Picking her up, Ingrid stroked her satiny coat affectionately and murmured something soft and sweet into her ear. Then, gently putting her down again, she went out into the foyer. As Joel watched her shapely figure disappear down the hall, he wondered if Ingrid had any idea how attractive she was. Probably not, he thought as, reluctantly, he tore his attention away from Ingrid and began to build the fire. Gussie wandered over to observe, her little black eyes blinking sleepily.

Reaching out, Joel gave her an affectionate pat on the head. "Lucky dog," he murmured.

Chapter Seven

After Joel had set up the table near the fire, he and Ingrid both sat down and placed the Monopoly board between them. There was a time when Joel had liked the game, but after playing it a half dozen times, he found that it tended to be long and boring. He'd even heard of games that had lasted for two days, a terrible thought.

"Do you mind if I make a suggestion?" he asked. "The game will go much faster if we take the value of each die thrown and consider it a separate turn."

Ingrid frowned, perplexed. "I'm not sure I understand what you mean. Why don't you go first and show me?" she suggested, handing him the dice.

"All right." Shaking the dice, Joel rolled a three and a six. "Now, first I'll take my six, that's Oriental

Avenue. I'll buy it. Then my three, which is Connecticut Avenue. See?" Hurriedly he slid his token across the board. "You can buy two pieces of property with one throw of the dice. It's your turn."

"Oh, now I understand," Ingrid said as she let her gaze roam leisurely over the board. "I can see where that would speed up the game, but why the rush? The reason we're playing is because we don't have anything else to do."

"I'm not rushing, but I do think we ought to keep the game moving. It's your turn."

Ingrid picked up the dice and shook them. "Don't hurry me. It's like making instant coffee so you can dawdle for an hour." Again she shook the dice, and shook them . . .

"Come on, throw!"

"All right, all right." The dice bounced onto the table and Ingrid leaned forward to inspect them. "Oh, two twos."

"That's a pair of snake eyes. Takes you to Community Chest and income tax where you owe an automatic two hundred dollars. But you also get to draw a card. Here, the yellow one."

Sighing patiently, Ingrid slid him a warning glance. "Look, I'm perfectly capable of moving my own token and drawing my own card. Now why don't you sit back and relax a little?"

"I'm only trying to help."

"How much help do I need to draw a yellow card?"

"You're a feminist."

"You're a chauvinist. And now that the pleasantries are over, do you mind if I draw my own card?" Without waiting for his reply, Ingrid picked one up and read it carefully and then pulled her brow into a frown. "Hmmm, I have to pay a school tax of a hundred and fifty dollars." Putting the card down, she started counting out the money. "I'm not sure I like this game. I've paid out three hundred and fifty dollars on my first throw and I have absolutely nothing to show for it. On the other hand, you've paid out . . ."

"Two hundred fifty and I own two pieces of property. You get another throw."

"Oh, that's right." Ingrid threw again, and again she got doubles, this time threes, which moved her to Chance where she drew a "Go Directly To Jail" card.

"That's rotten luck, Ingrid, but your other three would have gotten you there anyway," Joel consoled her as he scooped up the dice.

His luck held up throw after throw, while Ingrid's went from bad to worse. In less than an hour she was down to her last hundred dollars while Joel had fifteen pieces of property and seven hotels.

"Sure is a nice, exciting game," Ingrid remarked dryly. "And I give up. You can have everything but this hundred dollar bill. I'm going to keep it to remind me not to play Monopoly with you again."

"But don't you think playing like this makes the game much more alive and exciting?"

"Not particularly."

"Want to play another game the regular way?" Joel

wasn't ready to let Ingrid go yet. She was a fun person to be with, especially when she grumbled over her bad throws all the time. He knew she was just kidding, keeping the game going, playing the role of perfect hostess to a rather petulant guest. He admired her for this. In fact, he was finding Ingrid Christian to be a very unusual and interesting woman with a wide range of talents that spread from truck driver to artist to a seductress with big brown eyes and a slow sensuous smile that absolutely captivated him.

Pushing her chair back, Ingrid folded her hands in her lap. "I think I've had enough Monopoly for one afternoon."

"What do you usually do on weekends?" he asked as he got up to stoke the fire.

"I'm not a hermit, if that's what you mean. I have many friends who are also single, and we go out to dinner, movies, plays and various activities at school. Then, of course, my family's close by, so we visit back and forth."

"Ever travel?"

"No. Unfortunately, I've never had the time for that. My very big dream is to go around the world someday."

Joel put the poker back on its hook and sat down again. "That's a very big dream, all right, but not an impossible one."

Ingrid glanced up, her dark eyes reflecting the flames of the fire. "And how about you?" she asked. "What do you do on weekends?"

"I'm often out of town, but when I'm in New York, I'm usually involved with business dinners."

"Even on Sunday?"

"No. I go to the gym on Sunday to get the kinks out before I have to tackle another week."

"Mmmm." She eyed him critically. "Don't you ever take some time off and just relax?"

Joel shook his head. "Not often," he admitted. "At this point in my life, I'm still growing, spreading out, building a reputation. I can't afford to take time off and just goof around. But maybe in a couple of years or so, I'll be established enough to be more selective with my clients and just take the cases that interest me. Then I'll take it easy."

Ingrid shook her head. "I doubt that. You're not the take-it-easy type, and I should know. I was married to one for five years."

Joel's glance sharpened. Was she comparing him to her former husband? Was she fitting the faults of one onto the body of another? "Are you implying that I'm working myself up to a heart attack?"

"It's been known to happen," she answered quietly.

"Don't forget," Joel reminded her, "Rob had heart trouble all his life."

Her brows lifted. "And you're as healthy as a mule?"

"As a bucking bronco," he corrected.

Ingrid's face widened into an easy smile. "Have it your way. I suppose bucking broncos can be stubborn, too."

"I'm not stubborn," he argued. "I'm just persistent."

"Good," she said, getting to her feet, "then you can pursue the goal of getting dinner on the table again. You did so well yesterday."

"Is it that time?"

Ingrid swung her glance to the wall clock in the hall. "It's five-thirty. I'll make a deal with you. If you take Gussie out, I'll get the ice cubes."

Joel sprang to his feet. "You're on," he said. "Come on, pooch, let's move."

As Joel followed Ingrid out to the foyer, he put a hand on her shoulder. When he turned toward the hallway leading to the snow room, he gave it an extra squeeze and delighted at the shivering response beneath his fingers. Ingrid glanced up at him, her lips parted in a slight smile that sent tremors down his spine. At that moment, she looked more beautiful than he had ever seen her. As if sensing his reaction, Ingrid turned abruptly and went into the kitchen, but not in time to hide the look of fondness that appeared on her face, a look that made Joel's pulse leap and his hopes soar.

God, he thought as he tromped off to the snow room, if he didn't work off some of this steam, he was going to make an ass of himself.

The cold snap of winter swirled around him, but the brisk coolness felt good against his cheeks. Inhaling deeply, Joel made his way to the garage for the snow shovel. What he needed was a good workout, something that would leave him physically exhausted. Within minutes he was diligently shoveling the path leading from the house to the truck. For the first time in his thirty-six years, he realized the phenomenon of being at the mercy of an uncontrollable force and found it strangely exciting to find himself alone against the forces of nature with nothing but a shovel between him and his destiny.

Well, he admitted as he sent the snow flying through the air, he was fantasizing a little. He seemed to be doing a lot of that lately. Maybe it was because he'd been away from the city for several days and his mind thought it was on a holiday. God knows, it deserved it. In the six years he'd been with Stanley Carmichael's law firm, he'd never taken a decent vacation. He'd snatched a few days now and then, but there was always an important case on the agenda that demanded the skill and resources of everyone in the firm.

When he had shoveled his way to the truck he stopped and watched his breath hang in the air for a few moments. He could have gone on for another half hour, should have gone on for another half hour, but the vision of the lovely Ingrid waiting for him inside changed his mind. To hell with the workout. After all, he didn't want to go back in there a physical cripple, did he?

Brushing the snow from the windshield of the truck with a quick sweep of his arm, Joel's gaze swept to the barn where Ingrid kept her car. Then he looked at the garage where she kept the hay and feed. He shook his head, perplexed. He still hadn't figured that one out. Maybe he'd better hurry inside and ask Ingrid.

This time he didn't call to Gussie to hurry up. He

scooped her up in his arms and ran up the walk and into the house.

While Ingrid arranged olives on a relish plate, Joel stood in front of the freezer with the door wide open. For a full five minutes, he'd taken packages of frozen food out, read the labels describing their contents and put them back in again.

"Look," Ingrid said, "if I'd wanted to turn this kitchen into an igloo, I'd have opened the window."

"Just taking inventory. Like to know where I stand."

"You're standing in front of the freezer. Any turkey could tell you that."

"All right. All right." Tossing a package of peas back onto the shelf, he closed the door. "Besides, I'm all finished."

"Then why don't you go into the living room and make out your inventory report while I get the dinner?"

Coming up behind her, Joel circled his arms around her waist and deliberately pressed his body into hers. Ingrid exhaled a long, audible sigh. "We went over this subject this afternoon and we both decided it could only lead to a dead end."

"Both? I don't remember agreeing to anything as ridiculous as that."

"It was more or less understood."

He planted a kiss in the soft hollow behind her ear. "It seems to me we were talking about physical attraction and vibes."

Pulling away from him, Ingrid started fussing with

the salad. "True, but we also have to face reality. After tomorrow, we'll probably never see each other again."

"But why waste today because of what might happen tomorrow?"

"I can see there's no reasoning with you," Ingrid said with a shake of her head. "So we won't even discuss it."

"I don't want to discuss it anyway. I want to—"

"Roquefort, French, or Thousand Island?"

"You're changing the subject. You are also denying a strong potent male animal who, in the prime of his sexual prowess, is—"

"Ready for a drink?"

"Oh, I suppose so," he said in defeat. "How about you? A double?"

"No, no, just a small one."

"I think you need a double."

"One."

"Why don't you unwind, let yourself go, like you did this afternoon?" He clamped his hands on her shoulders in a firm, intimate grip.

Ingrid had to swallow the rising lump in her throat. "I don't want to hear any more about this afternoon."

"Neither do I. I just want to relive it."

"Well, forget that. My response was a spontaneous reaction to a situation that, well, that . . ." She fumbled for the right words, but they just weren't there. "Anyway, my impulsiveness was more or less the consequence of a series of, ah, of . . ." He made her so nervous, standing there staring at her, that she could hardly talk. "Of, um, circumstances where the . . ." Her voice trailed away into a befuddled silence.

"Maybe you'd better take the double."

"I think you're right."

To celebrate the fact that they had mastered another delicious meal, Ingrid and Joel treated themselves to big cups of Irish coffee topped with whipped cream. Ingrid settled herself in one corner of the couch, her feet tucked under her, her hand across the back of the sofa, her head resting on her arm. Dreamily she watched the fire while Joel watched her. It wasn't long, however, before he completed his silent scrutiny and moved in for a closer study. Sliding beneath her outstretched arm, he placed his hand around her waist and, gathering her into his arms, hugged her to him like a big, friendly bear.

In spite of her resolve, Ingrid found herself melting into the arms that wrapped around her like a warm blanket. She couldn't pretend not to be affected by the gentleness of his touch, the strength of his body next to hers, the easy rhythm of his breath in her hair. Nor could she pretend that she wasn't aware of the sexual awakening of her body, something that had been missing from her life for a long time.

Ingrid knew the dangers of an intimate relationship with Joel. She also knew her defenses were in a very precarious position. She'd almost reached the point of abandoning all restraint and enjoying the pleasures of the moment. Almost. But not quite. Fortunately, a few shreds of propriety remained coupled with the knowledge that if she gave in to her desires, she would be left to face the jaws of loneliness tomorrow. Because then

Joel would leave her, just as Rob had, and once again she'd be left alone.

As though sensing her inner turmoil, Joel made no aggressive moves. He seemed content to just hold her in his arms and stare lazily into the flickering embers.

Without turning his head, Joel raised his arm and affectionately smoothed Ingrid's hair away from her face. "Do you ever get lonely out here?" he asked, his voice almost a whisper.

"Sometimes," she answered. "But then, doesn't everyone?"

"I guess so. I just never thought about it. They say you can be lonely in a room full of people. But way out here it's so remote."

"Everyone tells me that," she said. "I suppose I should sell this place and move into an apartment, but I'm just not ready for that yet. I still love the open country and all the serenity that goes with it."

"Then keep it," he advised. "If this is where your roots are, then this is where you should stay."

Leaning her head back against his arm, Ingrid studied him for a long moment. Then, quietly, she asked, "Where are your roots?"

"Fortunately, I don't have any," he answered quickly. "I'm free to go wherever I want, whenever I want."

When Ingrid offered no response to this, Joel shifted his gaze to hers, and for many long moments their eyes locked in a silent appraisal of each other. Then, gently, he tipped her head back and kissed the tip of her nose, and then her eyelids. His mouth closed over hers in an almost featherlike kiss, but there was no mistaking the insistence that was there nor the throb of desire that smoldered just below the surface.

Ingrid could feel her body relax, melt into his as if they'd been together always. Even the pleasant shiver of warmth seemed familiar, but as he gathered her closer, something changed. The kiss deepened with a tantalizing invitation for more, and Ingrid, with reckless disregard of the warning voice that whispered in her head, cast the shadows aside and let her heart lead her to the delights her body coveted.

As her senses throbbed with excruciating awareness, she moved her hands over the corded muscles of his chest to the back of his head. Gently, she massaged the tendons in his neck in a slow rhythmic motion that matched the circular movement of his lips as they moved over hers.

A gentle moan of contentment escaped her, and, willingly, she parted her lips and allowed him to possess her mouth and explore its inner softness. His touch was as light as it was tormenting, and Ingrid became aware of a new sensation, a sweet aching heat spreading through her whole body.

"Hmmm," Joel murmured as his lips trailed kisses across her cheek. "You taste good." The kisses continued on their path down the side of her neck to the edge of her collar. "Smell good, too." She felt his hand cup her breast and hold it like a fragile ornament. "And feel wonderful." Exhaling a long, ecstatic sigh, Ingrid folded her arms around his head and held him even closer.

Suddenly she stiffened. Sitting straight up, Ingrid

stared into the darkness, every nerve taut as she listened. Then she heard it again, something far in the distance, something that swept through her like a cold wind. She tried to pretend it wasn't there, that it didn't matter anyway, but in that moment an emotion stronger than passion gripped her with gnawing dread.

"What's wrong?" Joel asked, startled by her sudden rigid pose.

"Listen!" she whispered, her voice barely audible.

Together they sat in the silence, their ears straining into the night. And then it came again, the rumbling throb of heavy equipment.

A shiver shook her body. "The snowplows," she said under her breath.

"They're clearing the roads?" His voice held a note of surprise.

She nodded, but she couldn't speak. The realization that tomorrow he would be gone forever was too much for her to bear.

"But the planes probably won't be flying," he said.

He seemed to regret his departure as much as she did—a small consolation, but a cherished one. "Oh, I'm sure they will be," she murmured as she pulled out of his arms and straightened her shoulders. Then, with a tremendous effort, she summoned forth every ounce of pluck in her body and stood up.

"Where are you going?" Joel asked, surprised.

"I think we'd better put the brakes on this relationship," she stated, trying to keep the tremor out of her voice.

Joel blinked, disbelieving. Then he, too, rose. "What

are you talking about? We're just getting to know each other."

Carefully, Ingrid smoothed her sweater into place. "We're also getting carried away."

"Well, what's wrong with that?"

Ingrid could almost feel her frustrations and resentments gathering together like a mighty force. Suddenly they all exploded in an uncontrolled outburst of anger. "Everything!" she shouted.

"That's a hell of an answer!"

"It's the only one you're going to get!" Spinning away from him so he wouldn't see the tears in her eyes, she ran from the room.

Once Ingrid was in her bedroom with the door closed firmly behind her, she fought hard to keep the tears in check. Even now she was reluctant to admit how deep her feelings toward Joel were. What in hell was the matter with her, anyway? She'd known from the very beginning that their relationship would be short-lived. Then why was she allowing herself to enter the danger zone, that point of no return when you've lost your heart and have nothing more to give? That point where you can only wait and hope that your love will be returned?

Love? That was a strange word to associate with Joel Stires. Love was a mutual thing, something to be shared and cherished, and it came before all else. But Joel was a man without roots, a career man. He'd never let anything come between him and his continuing success. The only love he knew was challenge and conquest.

Despite her pep talk, Ingrid had trouble getting to sleep. It was late before she closed her eyes and late when she opened them the next morning. Jumping out of bed, she threw on some warm clothes, knowing she'd be outside most of the day, and started for the kitchen. As soon as she opened her bedroom door, the aroma of fresh-perked coffee wafted to her nostrils. She found herself smiling. She always kept the coffee in the freezer. Joel's inventory the previous day had paid off after all.

As Ingrid poured her coffee, she could hear Joel's voice coming from the study. He was on the phone, probably talking to Peter Moggs about transportation to the airport, she thought ruefully. When he hung up, he came into the kitchen with a broad smile plastered all over his face, all evidence of the previous evening's flare-up either concealed or forgotten. Uh-oh, she fretted as she stirred her coffee faster and faster.

Putting his hands on her shoulders, Joel kissed her affectionately on the cheek. It was just a brotherly gesture, she told herself, the type one exchanges in an airport at the departure gate.

"Well," he said, pulling some notes out of his pocket, "while you've been sleeping, your secretary has been hard at work. Let's see . . ." he was having trouble reading his own writing. "Oh, here. First of all, your mother called to wish you good morning and to tell you that your brother and your dad would be over later to clear the driveway."

Ingrid closed her eyes with exasperation. "It's so nice to have someone answer my phone for me while I sleep. Funny, though," she said, "I have a phone right next to my bed. I didn't hear it."

"Maybe that's because I caught it on the first ring. I was sitting right there making a few calls."

"Oh, really?" Who would he be calling? she wondered.

"First I called the airport to cancel my reservation, and then I called our firm's answering service to let them know that I have decided to take a few days off and enjoy the countryside."

Ingrid was so stunned she almost dropped her cup on the floor. "You what?" she cried.

"It's very simple," he explained matter-of-factly, "I'm going to spend some time here in the peace and quiet of . . . of . . . what's the name of this place, anyway?"

"Ohio."

"I know that. I'm talking about the town."

"Springland, but don't bother to remember it. You're not going to be here that long. In fact," she said, glancing up at the clock, "I would estimate your stay will terminate in about three hours."

"You're making rash judgments again, Ingrid," he informed her calmly. "But that's all right. I understand."

"No, I don't think you do. You cannot stay here another day, let alone several days. In case you've forgotten, I have classes to teach. I also have a family who will most assuredly . . ."

"Hold it right there," he cautioned, flinging his hands up in a halting gesture. "Would you just let me handle this? After all, I'm sure I don't have to remind you that my experience in dealing with matters of this nature is extensive and unequaled."

"Hogwash."

Suddenly he grinned. "Just promise me one thing, Ingrid. When your father arrives, let me handle him, all right? Do you think you could keep in the background for a few minutes while I smooth the road for us?"

"What do you mean, 'for us'?"

Cupping her head between his hands, he turned her face up to his. "I've decided you're right. We need more time together." She started to protest, but he hurried on. "And since you're so overly emotional, it will be up to me to handle the groundwork."

Ingrid shook her head, a slight smile on her lips. "Well, I'll tell you something, I'm not going to worry about it. When my dad gets here he'll throw you out."

Joel shook his head. "No, he won't. You have to realize that I'm capable of controlling any situation that might arise."

Ingrid eyed him skeptically, but before she could answer, she heard the sound of a truck driving down the road and looked out the window to see who it was. "There they are," she said.

When the heavy truck stopped at the end of the drive to lower the plow blade, Ingrid noticed there were three people in the front seat, which meant that her mother had come, too. Slowly the truck made its way up the drive, cutting a swath through the drifts and sending the snow spewing to the side like a fountain. When it stopped at the end of the walk, her father got out on the passenger side and reached back to help her mother, a petite woman in her early fifties. She was carrying a covered box, and Ingrid knew she'd brought croissants, her favorite pastry.

As soon as they started up the walk, her brother, Kipp, who was driving, put the truck in gear and proceeded to clear a path to the barn. As Ingrid hurried to the door to let them in, she gave Joel a quick backward glance. "I hope your talk is as good as your confidence."

"Not to worry," he assured her.

Everyone stomped the snow off their boots and Ingrid introduced her parents, the Fentons, to Joel. Then she took the croissants while Joel hung up her mother's coat, helped her with her boots and marveled at the beauty of her Canadian ski sweater. Mrs. Fenton smiled politely and thanked him, but Ingrid knew she wasn't buying it. Her mother wasn't easily swayed by flattery and smooth manners.

Ingrid and her mother went to the kitchen while Joel stayed behind to make sure her father's needs were taken care of. Then the two men went into the living room, where they could talk.

Gussie greeted the new arrivals by wiggling her rump and licking their hands.

"Oh, my," Mrs. Fenton exclaimed as she picked Gussie up. "Kipp is going to love you."

"She's a beauty, all right." Ingrid poured two cups of coffee and set them on the table, then made another pot. "Come on, Mom, sit down and have a croissant."

"I don't need any more pastry, honey, but I'll take

the coffee and sit down." Ingrid detected the slight emphasis on the last two words and knew her mother was anxious to talk about Joel, the famous criminal lawyer from New York who was staying at her unmarried daughter's house for the weekend.

Therefore, Ingrid wasn't surprised when her mother opened the conversation with "He's terribly polite, isn't he?"

Ingrid smiled. Very little escaped her mother. "He was just putting on his best manners for your benefit," she confided. "Normally, he's a real pain in the neck."

"Is that right?" Her mother sipped her coffee. "For someone who's been saddled with a grouchy houseguest for two days, you seem to be in good spirits. Very good spirits, I might add." She eyed Ingrid over her cup. "Nice-looking man, too, hmm?"

Ingrid shrugged. "Yes, I suppose, in a rugged sort of way."

"Tall, confident, educated, a very personable man."

"Mmm," Ingrid murmured. She, too, had taken to sipping her coffee between sentences, a family trait designed to give one time to think before speaking.

"Very pleasant over the phone," her mother went on. Then she eyed Ingrid levelly. "Is he married?"

"No. Divorced."

"How nice."

Lowering her voice, Ingrid leaned closer. "Look, Mom, he's just not my type. So forget it."

"All right. Have it your way. But I can tell that you're going to miss him when he leaves this afternoon."

Ingrid took a deep breath and leaned still closer. "Mom, that's what I wanted to explain. He's not leaving."

Two eyebrows shot up. "He's not? Why?"

"He's decided to stay a little longer and rest."

"Could you repeat that?"

"It's the truth. He informed me of this just before you got here."

"And how do you feel about it?"

"Well," Ingrid said, "I don't know. I suppose . . ."

"Never mind fumbling for an excuse, dear. I've got the picture." She laid an affectionate hand on Ingrid's arm. "And I'm not going to censure you. At age twenty-eight, you're quite capable of making your own decisions. But," she stated firmly, "that does not mean that I approve."

"I understand that, Mom, and I respect you for it, but I have to travel my own road."

"Of course you do, but," Mrs. Fenton cupped a hand to the side of her mouth to keep from being overheard, "you realize that your father will hit the ceiling, don't you?"

Closing her eyes, Ingrid nodded in agreement. Her dad was a wonderful person, but if he thought any man was trying to take advantage of his daughter, he wouldn't hesitate to act first and ask questions afterward. "I know," she said.

"Have you thought of how you're going to handle it?"

"No," she said, straightening her shoulders, "and frankly, I'm not going to worry about it. Since this was

Joel's idea, I'm letting him handle it. He keeps reminding me of how persuasive he is, so let's see a little evidence."

"All I can say is, I'm glad I'm here to see the fireworks. It's been a dull week."

"Not for me." Ingrid smiled dreamily. "In fact, I wouldn't trade these last few days for anything in the world."

Mrs. Fenton exhaled a long, tired sigh. "I don't know why you can't settle for a nice, quiet local boy."

Ingrid shook her head. "There are times, Mom, when I don't think you know me at all."

"There are times when I think you're right."

Chapter Eight

$\mathcal{K}$ipp, Ingrid's seventeen-year-old brother, finished shoveling out the driveway and tramped into the house with a loud, cheery hello. Ingrid called back, but Gussie bounded out to greet the new arrival. Immediately, Kipp squatted down on the floor and let Gussie tromp all over him while he tried to wrestle with her. It was a game they both enjoyed and caused more commotion than Mrs. Fenton cared to put up with.

"Why don't you two go outside with that?"

Without further prodding, they both stormed out of the house. Ingrid, watching them from the window, could hear Kipp's laughter as he and the dog tumbled into the drifts together. She smiled with satisfaction. Gussie had been so quiet that she'd been a little worried that she wouldn't get along with Kipp, but

evidently all Gussie needed was a little encouragement
and she could roughhouse with the best of them.

Ingrid took the coffee into the living room, where her
mother, fearful that she might miss some excitement,
had joined the men. As Ingrid served the pastries, her
father sighed expansively and gave her an affectionate
pat on the arm.

"Joel seems to be as familiar with oil and gas
exploration as you are, having grown up in a family that
talked about nothing else." He helped himself to a
croissant and leaning back, crossed one foot over his
knee and smiled proudly. "It seems that drilling in
Oklahoma isn't much different from drilling in Ohio.
And let me tell you something, if I were a young lawyer
like you, I'd get into oil and gas leaseholds. There's a
fortune to be made there."

Joel nodded, agreeing. "That's what I understand. In
fact, I'm almost tempted to stay over a few days and
look into it."

Ingrid swung a quick glance to her mother, who had
conveniently lowered her eyes to the floor, pretending
to study the carpet. Ingrid followed suit.

"Might as well," her father went on. "As long as you
have the time, take a few days and look around. You
never know when opportunity will knock."

Ingrid almost choked on the croissant. It was obvious
that her father wasn't too impressed with Joel's success
as a criminal lawyer. To him, the world started
and ended with oil drilling, and Joel had been clever
enough to detect this and use it as common ground

between them. Maybe she'd underestimated Joel after all, she mused. Maybe he was as good as he said he was. But then, she thought, no one could be that good.

Kipp came back with the dog and joined them, his cheeks ruddy from the cold romp in the snow. Gussie looked as though she was ready for another go, however, and stuck close to Kipp. Already she knew who her playmates were. They talked for almost an hour, with Joel expertly steering the conversation away from oil and to safer subjects such as the weather, the seminar and wildlife conservation. Evidently, Ingrid decided, his knowledge of oil drilling was a little sparce and, since he'd made his point and won her father's respect, it was time to shift subjects. Mrs. Fenton asked a few questions here and there, but it was quite apparent, at least to Ingrid, that she was more interested in Joel's maneuvering than the subject at hand. She made no indication that she thought Joel's decision to stay over a few days to investigate the legal potentials in the area was based on anything but the most scrupulous of principles.

The guests were in their coats and standing at the door ready to leave when Mr. Fenton turned to Joel with an outstretched hand. "Remember," he said, "we always have an extra room at our house. If Ingrid doesn't treat you right, feel free to move in with us."

Joel thanked him politely. "I just might do that."

Suddenly Mr. Fenton's face split into a wide smile.

"Now, if I believed that, I'd believe almost anything, wouldn't I?"

"Howard!" his wife expounded.

"It's all right, Mrs. Fenton," Joel assured her with an easy smile. "I'm glad we understand each other."

"So am I," she agreed. Firmly she clasped her husband's arm and started nudging him toward the door. "Come on, you big lunk, before you embarrass all of us."

Her husband shrugged, unperturbed. "I'm not embarrassed. Are you, Joel?"

"Not in the least."

"Ingrid?"

"Yes!"

"See?" her mother scolded. "I told you. Now let's get going before they throw us out."

Laughing, he followed her out of the house and down the walk to the truck, where Kipp and Gussie were waiting. When Ingrid finally closed the door behind them, Joel turned to her with a big triumphant smile. "Did I win that case or didn't I?"

Ingrid just shook her head. "Too bad the legal profession doesn't have a 'Best Actor of the Year' award. You'd have won it hands down."

"I'm glad to see you appreciate my talents. And now," he said, slapping his hands together, "what are we going to do for the rest of the day?" The implication was obvious.

"We're going to get our snow clothes on and go out and feed the wildlife again."

Slumping his shoulders, Joel dropped his chin on his

chest in a gesture of abject defeat. "This is inhumane . . ."

When Joel saw that Ingrid was determined to go back outside and plow through the snow again, his resistance dissolved. Not only did he want to be with her every moment of the day, but he found himself liking the hikes in the woods. He could see how a man like Rob Christian had gotten caught up in his wildlife program.

He was also beginning to see why a woman as lovely and talented as Ingrid had chosen to remain in a small town like Springland, Ohio. It wasn't the beautiful home her husband had built for her or the wilderness or her teaching job, it was the strong family ties. They were almost like shackles, he thought, and wondered if she realized this. He glanced down at her. She was walking with a long, sure stride, her arms swinging, her red cap pushed back from her face at a jaunty angle. She certainly didn't present the picture of one who was tied down against her will, but more of one who had the security of deep roots, something Joel knew little about.

"Oh, look." Ingrid pointed suddenly. "There's an opossum behind that rock." Immediately she dropped her hay and feed on the ground and opened the box of graham crackers she'd brought along for a special treat. "Now be quiet," she whispered as she slowly approached the rock, holding out a cracker to the suspicious animal.

"Come on, Bandit," she murmured encouragingly.

The little black, beady eyes shifted from cracker to

stranger and back again and then waited until Ingrid threw the cracker onto the ground.

Joel watched, fascinated. "He sure looks big," he whispered.

"Oh, they get bigger than this. Bandit probably weighs about twenty pounds, but I've seen them half again as big."

"Are you trying to train him to be a pet?"

"Oh, no, never," she said as Bandit greedily grabbed the cracker and stuffed it in his mouth, his claws almost as dextrous as human hands. "When you teach a wild animal not to fear man, you make him very vulnerable. Opossums, however, are impossible to domesticate, so that's why I've allowed myself to pamper Bandit a little. He's been meeting me at this feeding station for almost three years now."

"Have you ever petted him?"

"Never. He may look friendly, but he has slashing claws and needle-sharp teeth and doesn't mind using them. Besides," she said, taking another cracker from the box, "why try and tame a wild animal?"

Why indeed? Joel asked himself as his gaze shifted to Ingrid. She was wearing a desert tan leather jacket with a sheepskin lining, tight-fitting ski pants and calf-high boots. Though her clothes were all in earthy tones, designed to blend with the landscape, Joel assumed, there was an elegance about Ingrid that couldn't be camouflaged. No matter where she was or what she was doing or how she was dressed, there was an aura of refined dignity about her that was as hard to define as it was to overlook.

Reluctantly, Joel had to admit that Ingrid, with a lifetime of country living, was very much at home in the woods, at ease in her surroundings. Even the blizzard had left her unperturbed. She had the confidence of one who'd learned to roll with the punches and could take almost anything nature offered. A valuable trait, he thought, and an unusual one in a woman as delicate and sensuously provocative as Ingrid.

Suddenly she stood up and brushed the crumbs from her gloves. The movement startled the opossum, who ran up a big oak tree and, settling on one of the largest branches, proceeded to glare down at them. Ingrid raised her eyes and scowled back. Then lifting her eyes very high, she seemed to smile into the sky. At that moment, Joel's feeling toward her was so intense that he felt an immediate desire to possess her. And it frightened him a little. She was unlike any woman he'd ever known and this time he wasn't as sure of his ground as he usually was. Ingrid was so different, gentle but direct. He liked that. In fact, he was beginning to like everything about her. It was too bad their worlds were so far apart, but he'd been over that before.

He'd lain awake most of the night thinking of Ingrid. Was there any future for them? he'd asked himself over and over. Would she ever be able to cut loose from her roots here and learn to adjust to a life in the city? Could she survive the clamor and noise and fast pace of New York? It'd be such a tremendous change for her and, deep down, he doubted if she'd be happy there. And yet Ingrid was a versatile, adaptable, intelligent woman. For all he knew, she might be dying to get out of Springland and into a new life-style. It was this thread of hope that had caused him to decide to stay over for a few more days. If there was any possibility, however remote, that they could make it together, he was not going to let it slip through his hands.

Joel realized suddenly that Ingrid had been looking at him for several minutes. He could almost feel her thoughts as she studied him with that quiet expression of hers that he was finding more and more irresistible. Meeting her gaze, he caught her eyes and held them, and in that moment the invisible link between them seemed to lock into place.

A flicker of a smile rose at the edge of Ingrid's mouth that said more than words. Wrapping his arms around her, he hugged her to him and felt her arms clasp his body. Then they both squeezed at the same time and laughed at their silliness. Picking up the empty hay bags, they started back to the house, holding hands and swinging their arms back and forth like children, laughing and talking and bumping into each other. And giggling like two people in love.

"Why don't we take the truck and go into the thriving metropolis of Springland?" Ingrid suggested as they neared the house. "We could leave right after you fix lunch and clean up the kitchen."

"Is that the only entertainment you have to offer?" The suggestion was obvious.

"No. We could build a snowman and go sledding down the back hill."

His optimism knew no limits. "What else?"

"I could take you over and introduce you to Laura and Peter Moggs. They're dying to meet you."

"What else?"

"You can help me clean out the hall closet or work on your papers or watch TV."

He shook his head, amused at her deft evasion of the topic that was uppermost in both their minds. "Let's just work on the lunch first and go from there." There was always the hope that she'd change her mind by the time the meal was over.

"Good idea," she said as she tugged off her boots and walked, stocking-footed, down the hallway toward the foyer. She turned to him with a smile. "Anything you fix will be fine. I'll be right back, just want to get out of these heavy ski pants and get into something more comfortable."

"Really?"

"Like my jeans."

"Oh." He sounded disappointed, but he went into the kitchen, good sport that he was, and started opening cupboard doors. The issue of lunch was farthest from his mind. Plans for reviving the shared moments that had ended so abruptly last night were foremost in his thoughts. Ideas for approaching the subject and, not incidentally, conquering it, began to take form.

Suddenly Ingrid appeared in the doorway of the kitchen, a perplexed look on her face. "Where's my phone?"

"Oh, the phone." He snapped his fingers. "I forgot all about it."

"Forgot? What do you mean forgot? Where is it? How did you get it?"

He raised a cautioning hand. "Please, one question at a time."

"Stop stalling!"

"It's in the study."

"It is?" She blinked, amazed. "How did it get there?"

"I carried it there in my hand," he stated honestly. "You see, while you were still sleeping this morning, your mother called, but fortunately for you, I caught it on the first ring and it didn't wake you up. Then I got to thinking that someone else might call or she might call back, and I knew you wouldn't want to be disturbed, so I tiptoed into your room, unplugged the phone and took it . . ."

"You came into my room while I was asleep?" She stepped back, her eyes wide with astonishment. "You dared to barge into—"

"I didn't barge. I knocked softly, and when you didn't answer, I tiptoed in."

Tilting her head to one side, she eyed him suspiciously. "And just how softly did you knock?"

"Very." He gave her one of his slow, secret smiles. They'd never failed him yet.

"That," she said, mincing her words, "is invasion of privacy."

"If you say so, but remember, you were a party to it. If you didn't want me in your room, you should have locked the door."

"I was so upset last night, I forgot."

"And I forgot to knock, so we're even." Teasingly, he brushed the back of his hand across her cheek. "Now, do you want the phone back or do you want to stand here and argue about it?"

She sighed resignedly. "Just give me the phone."

"Coming up."

Brushing past her a little closer than was necessary, he went to the study and returned moments later carrying the phone. But instead of giving it to Ingrid, who stood waiting, he turned down the hall toward her room. He'd expected her to follow, to supervise the installation; when she didn't, he was a little surprised and very disappointed, but not defeated. He plugged the phone in and checked the dial tone. Then, carefully, he withdrew the plug just enough to disconnect the dial tone and sat down on the edge of her bed. It was still unmade and looked deliciously comfortable with its puffy quilt and flowered sheets. He ran his hand over a soft pillow and gently patted it.

"This phone doesn't work!" he bellowed. "No dial tone."

As he'd expected, Ingrid voiced a few terse phrases of accusation and came striding down the hall.

"You probably don't have it turned on," she said and after walking over to the bed, she took the phone from Joel's hands. "See? There's an on/off button here on the side." She pushed it to "on" and listened. "There's no dial tone," she murmured, perplexed. Glancing at the wall to make sure it was plugged in, she tried again.

Joel moved over a little to give her some room and, almost automatically, she sat down beside him, and pushed the button to "on" again and then "off." Leaning against her to look over her shoulder, Joel could smell the faint scent of roses in her hair. Brushing his face against her ear, he planted a warm, moist kiss on her cheek. "Mmm, you smell like a flower garden," he murmured, putting his arm around her shoulders to pull her a little closer. He could feel her slight shudder of arousal and knew that the hot fire of desire he felt was coursing through her, too.

She pulled away slightly, still reluctant to give herself to him. "I think you broke this thing on purpose," she said, trying to sound serene and unruffled but not succeeding.

His grip tightened and, wrapping both arms around her neck, he tipped her head back until their lips were inches apart. "Maybe I can fix it later."

"Later?" she murmured, her breathing ragged and hot against his cheek.

"Much later," he whispered as he kissed the moist hollow of her throat. Then, moving upward to her mouth, his lips locked with hers in the hungry search for fulfillment that had been building in both of them since the moment they'd met. To Joel's delight, Ingrid's arms slid around his neck while his own hands were free to roam wantonly down the smooth curves of her body, over the soft mounds of her breasts and downward to her waist, where he slid a hand beneath the belt of her ski pants.

"Let's get out of these things," he whispered huskily.

He felt Ingrid hesitate for a moment, but pretended not to notice and, pulling her blouse out of her pants, he skimmed a hand up and across her ribcage, spreading his fingers so that his thumb touched the outline of her breast in a tantalizing invitation for more. Her response was a soft sigh that seemed to come from someplace far away, and then she was unbuttoning her blouse with trembling fingers. Suddenly she stepped out of her pants, tossed the rest of her clothes onto a chair and, with a teasing laugh, dove under the blankets and pulled them up to her chin.

"For someone so anxious, you're sure slow."

"You have to allow for a moment of stunned realization," he said as he threw the last of his clothing aside and tumbled into bed beside her.

They lay cuddled together, their naked bodies burning with the heat of the excitement that shimmered between them. Joel reveled in the delicious feel of her flesh against his and sensuously rubbed her back and shoulders and explored the soft lines of her waist, her hips, her upper thighs. Then, moving to the front, he gently outlined the circle of her breasts. Ingrid took a quick intake of breath at the intimacy of his touch. He felt her body relax as though succumbing to the desire possessing her, carrying her to the ultimate satisfaction her body craved.

A stab of intense yearning filled him with a passionate ache that demanded fulfillment. Teasingly, his tongue trailed a path around the side of her breast before his lips captured a rosy nipple and suckled gently. He could feel Ingrid's body surge as currents of desire raced through her, a desire that triggered a new urgency in his own body. All he wanted to do was crush her to him and let the flood of rapture carry him to the ultimate height.

"Let's stay here forever," he murmured.

Her answer was a long, sensuous sigh and a tightening of her arms as she snuggled deeper into his embrace, making the closeness between them new and wonderful and intense.

Still cupping one hand around the nape of his neck, Ingrid moved the other across the plane of his back with deliberately sensuous movements. She worked her fingers down his spine to his waist and then, slowly, seductively, she lowered them to his firm, round buttocks and began a deep, circular massage that sent his level of desire shooting upward with every stroke.

"Oh, God, that feels good," he groaned with pleasure. "You have talents I never dreamed existed."

"I want to surprise you," she whispered, still massaging, still firing him with passion and filling him with incredible spasms of untamed desire.

And then he felt her body shift, her legs spread, her thighs tighten against his sides. Holding himself off with muscle-corded arms, he looked into her face. Her eyes were sparkling with an inner fire that was filled with a passion and expectation that matched his own. With deliberately slow movements, he circled his arm around her hips, cupped a hand under her buttocks and raised her body to his. She responded by wrapping her legs around him, drawing him closer, pressing his stomach onto hers.

And then, as Joel let his weight descend, he felt her body open to him, eager, inviting. As he entered with sure, deep thrusts, a gasp of pleasure escaped her lips. Arching into him, she joined his feverish body in a throbbing rhythm of their own making. Totally meshed together, the ecstasy of their union increased in tempo, their bodies became fire-hot, their breath jagged and irregular.

Suddenly, in a hard, fierce final encounter, Joel clasped her to him. As the ecstasy of radiant passion exploded all around them, they crashed together in a tremendous, shuddering climax that carried Joel beyond the wilderness of desire and into a sphere of total satisfaction that only Ingrid could give him.

As they slowly drifted back down to earth, Ingrid clung to him, her slender body damp and still trembling with the passion that had carried them both to hitherto-unknown levels of fulfillment.

As Ingrid curled into his arms, he could feel her body start to relax. Dreamily, she raised her eyes to his. "That was wonderful," she murmured contentedly.

His grip tightened momentarily. "And so are you," he whispered.

Smoothing a strand of hair away from Ingrid's brow, he looked deep into her face. Her eyelids were beginning to flutter shut, the long lashes like fringe on her cheeks. As her breathing began to return to normal, he could feel her body relax as a small smile of contentment touched the corners of her mouth. Even in sleep, she was something special.

Unlike Ingrid, however, Joel's eyes didn't close. Though he felt exhausted and deliciously fulfilled, disturbing thoughts jumbled his mind, the foremost being how swiftly their relationship had changed from that of total strangers who enjoyed sparring, joking, teasing to that of lovers. His heart ached with a longing that couldn't be fulfilled.

The realization that his relationship with Ingrid could possibly come to an abrupt halt as soon as he returned to New York was a painful one for him to accept. If she didn't want to go with him, he tried telling himself that someday he'd come back for her. But would it work? Since he'd been working with Stanley Carmichael's firm, his career occupied all his time and energy. At this point in his life, he was just beginning to emerge as a renowned criminal lawyer. From here on in, the cases he took would be big ones in the hundred-thousand-dollar range and up. This was the goal he had strived for since he left the public defender's office seven years before to begin his education with Stanley Carmichael. It would be a tragedy to falter now or change directions.

Yet a thread of optimism still remained. It all rested with Ingrid. If her feelings toward him were as strong as his were toward her, what was to keep her from leaving Springland? Suddenly he stopped himself and shook his head. What was the matter with him? He'd just gone all over that. His thoughts were beginning to go round and round. What he needed was a nice nap followed by a long, hot bath.

Closing his eyes, he started with the nap.

Chapter Nine

When Ingrid awoke less than an hour later, sunlight was streaming into the room. With a lazy yawn, she let her eyes adjust to the light and then, suddenly remembering where she was, she turned her head to the sleeping man beside her. Joel had the sheet pulled partially over his muscular body, leaving just his broad chest and shoulders and long, powerful arms exposed. Letting her eyes roam leisurely over his beautifully proportioned body, Ingrid took the time to study him in this most unusual pose of relaxation and tranquillity.

The strength of Joel's features, especially his square jaw, were softened, now, by the slightly parted lips, the closed eyes with the reddish lashes and the ruffled, sandy-brown hair that fell across his forehead in a disorderly swath. In sleep, he looked much younger, she thought, but awake or asleep, he was absolutely magnificent and she found herself longing to hold him, to feel his strong arms around her, his legs pressing against hers.

But enough! If she had any brains she wouldn't even be here. Yet, the romantic in her argued, if you can handle the consequences, why not enjoy the moment and to hell with tomorrow?

Carefully, Ingrid slid out of bed and tiptoed quietly to the bathroom. She snapped on the lights out of habit and immediately turned them off again. With the sunlight streaking through the large windowpanes, the room was already deluged with a dazzling blur of romantic colors. Only the verdant plants at the edge of the tub cast shadows on the floor. The rest of the room was flooded with pink-tinged sunlight that was almost as subtle and delicate as Ingrid herself.

Walking over to her large Roman tub, Ingrid turned on the water, tossed in several snow-white sponges and a generous portion of wild-rose-scented bath crystals. Wrapping a towel around herself sarong fashion, she stood at the edge of the tub and idly watched it fill. Delicious shudders were still coursing through her, not letting her forget for a minute the compelling magnetism of Joel's potency, the electricity of his touch, the vitality that still held her captivated. As she stepped into the tub and immersed herself up to her chin in the warm water, Ingrid looked at the wide expanse of emptiness around her and suddenly realized that for many days she had been envisioning Joel in the tub beside her.

The tub had been put in when the house was built,

but Rob had never taken a bath in it, preferring a quick, brisk shower to a long, leisurely bath. That left Ingrid the only one to ever use it, so she surrounded it with bottles of cologne and bubble bath and soft sponge pillows and neat rows of exotic plants. Rob used to kid her about it, telling her it looked more like a brothel than a country bathroom, but Ingrid didn't care. It was her one corner in the world that she didn't have to share with anyone.

As Ingrid's legs floated to the surface, she tucked a small pillow behind her head and exhaled a long sigh of contentment. Her eyes drifted to the windows, where a clear view of the countryside and the mauve-tinted sky of late afternoon lay sprawled before her. Her thoughts, not surprisingly, wandered back to the bedroom and to the handsome giant who was still sleeping in her bed, and she found herself yearning to have him beside her, to feel his skin, warm and wet, his body rubbing against hers, their legs sensuously entwined. She could almost feel the softness of her breasts nudging against him as she moved her hands up and down his torso in a slow, sensuous massage. And then when he, too, became filled with uncontrollable desire, she'd embrace him worshipfully and begin a lust-arousing exploration of his body that would build and build, flesh against flesh, man fusing with woman.

"Hey in there!" Joel called from the bedroom. His voice blended so wondrously with Ingrid's fantasies that for a moment she felt disoriented. Then, suddenly realizing how ridiculous her thoughts had been, she sat straight up and, grabbing soap and washcloth, began scrubbing herself vigorously. "You're a moron, you know that, don't you, Ingrid?" she grumbled to herself as she hurried with her bath.

"Are you going to stay in there all day?" came the impatient voice from the other room. She knew from the slightly muffled sound that he was still in bed. Good.

"Just be a minute," she called back.

There was a long moment of silence. Suddenly Joel appeared in the doorway, wearing absolutely nothing. "I'm joining you," he announced.

Ingrid turned her back to him. "Oh, no, you're not. I don't take baths with people I don't know very well."

"But, Ingrid, I'm the man you've just been sleeping with."

"I don't care who you are, I don't know you well enough."

"Oh God, and I thought I'd heard them all." Without waiting for her reply, he strode across the room and stepped into the tub, sliding down into the water beside her. His skin was wet and warm, and his body bobbed against hers, their legs entwined sensuously.

But though they splashed and played and teased, it wasn't until that night, when they shared Ingrid's bed again, that they enjoyed each other at leisure. As Ingrid lay in Joel's arms and caressed his naked body, he moved his hands over her breasts and hips and thighs in a lazily sensuous pattern that blotted out Ingrid's few remaining inhibitions. Returning the pleasure she was receiving, she tasted his body with feverish kisses and gasped with delight when his lips roamed over her soft breasts and his tongue teased their rosy peaks. Suddenly Ingrid felt an urgent rush of heat scorching through her and, circling Joel with her arms, she drew him even closer, molding her softness into his hard thighs, exulting at his vibrant response to the flame of desire that burned within both of them.

Heatedly, they traveled the sensuous path to fulfillment together, drifting, gliding, dipping, soaring. Finally, the ravishing ecstasy they were seeking suddenly culminated into a thunderous climax that burst all around them in a whirl of dazzling sensations.

Afterward, breathless and damp with spent passion, they clung to each other and journeyed back to the world where their dreams began, their pulses beating as one, their bodies filled with a sense of completeness, their hearts satisfied and at peace.

Ingrid awakened Joel the next morning by sitting down on the edge of the bed and passing a cup of hot coffee across his face. She gently blew the aroma toward his nostrils. His eyes opened almost instantly.

She set the cup on the night table and watched him wake up. "Do you know it's almost ten o'clock?"

"A.M. or P.M.?"

"A.M., of course."

"Oh, hell, I thought it was time to go to bed." He skimmed his hand across the silky smoothness of her coral satin nightgown. It had tiny lace straps and looked as delicate and serene as the woman who wore it. "Hmm, that feels good. Much better than the granny gown."

"But not very warm," she smiled. "I just put it on for

your benefit. I thought I'd throw a little glamour into your life."

"Oh," he nodded. "I appreciate that. Do you do something in it? I mean, dance or anything like that?"

"I hadn't thought about it, but maybe in the next day or so I'll come up with something."

He gave her a possessive pat on the fanny. "Make it something we can do together, like a tango."

"I don't know how to tango, and I'm sure you don't either."

"Well, don't worry," he said, giving her a moist kiss, "I'm sure I'll think of something we can do together."

She patted his cheek affectionately. "I've already thought of something. We have to go to the grocery store."

"Oh God," he said, collapsing back onto the pillows. "Why waste time on chores like that when we could be bathing?"

"Because we're all out of milk."

The straightforwardness of her answer brought a smile to Joel's mouth and, wrapping his arms around her, he pulled her on top of him. Obviously he was ready to begin the ritual again, but Ingrid knew better than to give in to his coaxing. They could very easily end up in bed all day. Laughing, she wiggled out of his arms and stood up.

She resorted to her classroom tone of authority. "If you don't hurry up and get dressed, you'll miss the whole day. It's beautiful outside. Even you will appreciate it."

Though Joel made the motions of one who was in a hurry, Ingrid noticed he was taking his time with his coffee, dawdling as long as possible. She knew he was hoping she'd get tired of waiting and start getting bathed and dressed, in which case, of course, he'd be there to assist her.

She smiled brightly. "To speed things up, why don't you bathe in your room, and I in mine?" Without waiting for his protest, Ingrid picked up her clothes and headed for the bathroom. She paused on the threshold to give him a fluttering farewell with her fingers, then closed the door and locked it.

"What is this?" Joel complained in a loud, plaintive voice. "Separation of the fittest?"

"It's expediency," she called through the door. "Now hurry up."

They decided to postpone the visit to the grocery store and try a little sledding instead. While waiting for Ingrid to get the sleds, Joel, who couldn't see the purpose of a garage if you didn't use it, put the truck into the barn, next to Ingrid's sleek silver-toned sports car. As he was idly looking around at the large, empty structure, he spied a small toboggan leaning against the wall. Though he'd never been on one before, he'd seen pictures of people racing them down a hill and it had looked like fun. Obviously, they were simple enough to operate. They didn't even have steering equipment. All one had to do was sit on it and ride down the hill.

"You can't just sit there and expect it to go," Ingrid

complained as Joel positioned the toboggan at the top of the hill and got on it. "You have to push it off to get it started."

"Well, all right." He was agreeable. "Why don't you get on it and get settled, and I'll push off and hop on back?" Without waiting for her reply, he started getting off.

"That's not as easy as . . ." she started. "Wait! Don't get off! Joel! Grab it. Quick!"

"Huh?" He turned around just in time to see the toboggan zip down the hill without them.

"Oh, damn," Ingrid groaned.

But Joel watched its descent with awe-struck fascination. "Look at that sucker go!" he marveled, wide-eyed. "Hurry up, Ingrid, go get it. I can't wait to be on it the next time it goes."

As Joel trudged up the hill dragging the toboggan behind him, Ingrid sat in the snow at the top of the hill, knees up, arms hugging her legs, watching his ascent.

Finally, a little out of breath, Joel reached the top and once again positioned the toboggan at the crest of the hill. He motioned for Ingrid to get on it. "Sit way up front, now, so I'll have plenty of room."

"All right," Ingrid said and dutifully moved forward a few inches.

Joel squatted down to get a good grip, then dropped to one knee for better leverage. "If my knowledge of physics is correct, a good send-off should take us halfway across the field."

Lifting the back end slightly to free it from the snow,

he got it moving. But, since he was determined to get a really good start, he pushed it harder and faster until it shot down the hill like a rocket, Ingrid the sole passenger. As soon as Ingrid realized she was underway alone, she turned her head and shouted a good-bye. But Joel didn't see her. He'd already slumped into the snow, a beaten man.

It wasn't until the next run that they finally got it all together. Ingrid sat in front and Joel behind, with his arms securely wrapped around her. With the wind whipping away their screams of delight, they slid across the snow with the speed of a deer. When they finally reached the bottom of the hill, they tumbled off the toboggan and rolled into the snow together, laughing like children.

As he turned to Ingrid, Joel's face was flushed with an excitement that equaled her own. They circled their arms around each other and kissed with an easy familiarity. Despite the thick padding of their clothes, Ingrid could feel the hard contours of Joel's body as well as his trembling response.

"Not bad at all," Joel smiled, running his hand across the front of her quilted parka. "Why don't we go inside so that I can examine the evidence without so much bulk between us?"

"You've done enough examining for one day," she said, laughing. "But I'll tell you what I will do. I'll race you up the hill."

"All right," Joel said in quick agreement. "And I'll bet you a bath together that I win."

"You sound very sure of yourself. Remember, you'll be pulling the toboggan."

"Hmmm . . ."

"With me on it."

Teasing, he knuckled her chin. "In that case, I'll bet I lose."

"In that case, we'll both walk. Come on," she said, jumping to her feet. "Let's try it again."

"Sounds great." He looked up the hill, where the toboggan tracks had made deep impressions in the snow. "If we follow the same path, we should be able to beat our own distance record."

As Ingrid brushed the snow from her clothes, a slight shadow crossed her face. "Stop racing with yourself," she said quietly. "You're on vacation, remember?"

Joel, detecting the solemn note in her voice, glanced at her quickly. Her large dark eyes were fastened on him. "I keep forgetting that. It's been so long since I've had a vacation, I can't remember how to act."

"I know."

Suddenly Ingrid shook herself, dismissing the subject with a blink of the eye. Her face broke into a bright smile and, circling her arm around him, she turned their footsteps toward the top of the hill. "How about a nice hike?"

"Do I have a choice?" he asked as he dropped his arm across her shoulders. They began the long trudge uphill, their bodies bumping together in a pleasantly familiar pattern.

It was midafternoon when they finally decided to call

it quits and put the toboggan away. It wasn't until they went into the house and collapsed on the living-room sofas that they realized how physically exhausted they were.

"I'll build a fire as soon as I recuperate," Joel said.

"And if I have the energy to walk to the kitchen, I'll make some sandwiches and mix us a drink."

"What you should do is replace this antique coffee table with a portable bar."

"That would really look nice, Joel."

They were both so tired they could hardly talk, and when the phone rang, they decided not to answer it. Neither of them was in any shape to walk the twenty feet into the study. But the caller was a persistent one who phoned back almost immediately. Finally Joel dragged himself to his feet and ambled into the study to answer it. It was Stanley Carmichael.

"What's this about a vacation?" he asked, his voice lightly teasing.

"I've decided I need some time off. Why? Is there something wrong?"

"And how!" Carmichael exclaimed. "You know Jalara, that Arab sheikh whose wife moved to California and filed a divorce suit against him?"

"I heard about it. Sure."

"Two days ago she was kidnapped, and they've taken Jalara into custody."

"You can't be serious. What grounds do they have?"

"Very flimsy, but Jalara isn't taking any chances. He's hired us to represent him."

"Smart man." Idly, Joel fingered the pen on the desk. "I suppose you're calling to tell me to go out there."

"No, I sent Cummings. At this stage he can handle it, but if the wife's body should turn up, then you and I will both step in."

"Do you think he's guilty?"

"I don't know. But it stands to reason that any attorney in California could have gotten him out on bail. Why would he contact us if he were innocent?"

"True," Joel agreed. "But as long as Cummings is handling that, I'll go back to my vacation."

"Well, there's one more thing. The prosecutor has come up with a surprise witness in the Canelli case. A woman who claims to have been a friend of his wife swears that Mrs. Canelli told her she felt as if her life were in danger."

"Felt as if!" Joel exclaimed. "What kind of evidence is that?"

"Exactly." He could almost see Carmichael nodding his head. "Nothing you can't shake out of her on cross-examination, but we do have to get together tomorrow or the day after at the latest."

"How about the day after the day after tomorrow?"

"You're pushing me, Joel."

"You're used to that."

"All right," he conceded reluctantly, "take a couple of days, but no more."

"You're pushing me, Carmichael."

He could hear Carmichael laugh as he murmured a good-bye and hung up.

Going back into the living room, he saw that Ingrid had gone to make drinks, so he built the fire and waited until she came back and cuddled down beside him. They lounged lazily, their bodies pressed together with familiar intimacy, and dreamily talked about tobogganing, the advent of the dinner hour and the possibility of skipping it altogether when the phone rang again. This time Joel jumped up right away and grabbed the receiver. It was Carmichael again. He bypassed the preliminaries. "Jalara's wife's body has just been found. He's being charged with murder. You'd better get yourself in here tomorrow. This is going to be a big media event, and we want to be ready."

"Tomorrow, hell!"

"Listen, son, there's a million bucks on this one. For that kind of dough, your vacation can wait."

Joel realized Carmichael was right. This was their big one, and he knew they couldn't stall much longer. "Okay," he agreed. "I'll be there sometime tomorrow."

"I'll be waiting."

From where Ingrid was sitting in the living room, she could hear Joel's side of the conversation very clearly, and she blatantly eavesdropped. Whatever silly hopes she'd had that Joel would resist the temptation to hurry back to his old life-style melted like snow on a warm day. Reluctantly, she reminded herself that this was the inevitable termination of their relationship, something she'd known would happen from the beginning. In the meantime they'd exchanged a bit of each other's worlds for a few precious days, days she'd remember forever.

Joel came striding back into the room with a quick step and casually dropped down on the sofa beside her. "I have to leave in the morning."

"I know," she answered quietly.

He turned to her, a little surprised. His blue eyes held her liquid brown ones. "You sound as if this was the end of the road for us."

"Well," she murmured, "isn't it?"

"God, I hope not," he exclaimed and, gently taking her face between his hands, he kissed her lightly on the lips. "As far as I'm concerned, I'm still on vacation, and this is just a brief interlude." His thumb eased down the line of her jaw and gently traced the outline of her lower lip. To Ingrid's relief, she saw a slight twinkle of amusement flash into his eyes. "What are you doing Friday?"

"Friday?" she repeated, her pulse leaping with hope.

"Yes, this Friday."

Ingrid's relief was so great that she wanted to leap up and shout with joy, but that would have taken her out of Joel's arms, and she didn't want that, ever. Half closing her eyes, she looked at him through a fringe of dark lashes. "Well, I don't know," she demurred. "Are you asking for a date?"

"Damn right I am. How about five o'clock? I can catch the two-thirty flight out of LaGuardia, be in Cleveland at three forty-five, pick up a rental car and arrive here in time to start the fire."

Ingrid wondered if the smile on her lips could possibly be as big as the one inside her. "I'll see if I can't squeeze you into my busy schedule," she whispered, and bringing his mouth to hers, she covered his lips in a kiss that caused something deep inside of her to curl with excitement. Not one to take anything calmly, Joel put a firm hand at the back of her neck and, parting her lips with his tongue, explored her hungrily.

As Ingrid felt the comfort of his arms around her, she sighed contentedly. Dreams weren't the only things that sometimes came true, she thought. Miracles did, too.

The following morning, Ingrid and Joel stood at the kitchen window with their arms around each other while they watched for Peter Moggs's car. Though Ingrid knew Joel hated to leave, she also knew he was anxious to get back to New York, where the action was. Strangely, she didn't feel as depressed over his leaving as she had thought she would. Joel had promised to call her that evening. Besides, he'd be back on Friday, and they could pick up where they left off, couldn't they? Though Joel hadn't said so, she was sure he loved her as much as she loved him. Her feminine instincts told her to proceed with caution, but she found herself already counting the hours until he'd be back, feminine instincts be damned.

Peter Moggs's blue sedan pulled into the driveway at exactly seven-thirty. He tooted and waved and they waved back. Joel took her in his arms for a farewell kiss.

"Keep the fires burning," he whispered huskily.

"I will," she promised.

And then he was gone, striding toward Peter's car

with a confident step. As Ingrid watched him go, she felt a well of pride spring up within her. His tall, athletic form moved with the easy grace of a long-distance runner's. He looked imposing and impressive in his exquisitely tailored suit and loose-fitting topcoat. The transformation from the bumbling tobogganer to a stunning, virile business executive was a little breathtaking, but comforting, too. Ingrid found her heart free of shadows but filled with a longing that would have to wait until the end of the week to be fulfilled.

Chapter Ten

Getting into her high-heeled boots and charcoal-gray chesterfield, Ingrid tugged on her leather gloves, gathered up her books and papers and started for Mount Traver. She took her car, a low-slung Corvette, and got there a half hour before her first class began. Her art students were slow settling down, all still discussing the weekend storm and their various modes of survival. But Ingrid, who'd been teaching there for four years, managed to settle them down and get on with the advertising posters.

She had a free period at ten o'clock and went into the teachers' lounge, where she and Laura Moggs met daily.

"Was he really as handsome as his picture?" Laura asked, eager for the lowdown on Ingrid's weekend activities.

"He sure was," Ingrid said dreamily. "And a perfect gentleman."

Laura cast Ingrid a suspicious glance. "Do I detect a note of wistfulness in your voice?"

"Well," Ingrid said, straightening a little, "we did have a nice time together considering the circumstances."

"What did you do?" Laura prodded.

Ingrid waved her hand vaguely in the air. "We took walks and filled the bird feeders and, ah . . . just, ah . . ."

"You don't have to explain. I understand." Laura smiled. "And I want you to know I'm thrilled to death for you."

"Now wait a minute," Ingrid cautioned. "Don't start jumping to conclusions. Admittedly, we're attracted to each other, but I'm not sure about any permanent commitments." She tried to make her voice sound slightly unconcerned. Ingrid and Laura had been friends since high school and knew each other well. Though Laura was a woman with a big heart, her imagination was even bigger. If she suspected how Ingrid felt toward Joel, she'd go out that very day on her lunch break and buy a wedding gift.

"What's wrong with permanent commitments?" Laura asked. "You're both single and that's the only requirement."

Ingrid shook her head. "I wish it was that simple, but I'm afraid there are a lot of stumbling blocks in front of us."

"The main one being . . ." Laura's voice trailed off expectantly.

"Our occupations for one thing. Our environments."

"Doesn't he like the country?"

"I think he likes it, but not on a permanent basis."

"And you don't like the city," Laura summarized as she leaned back in her chair to eye Ingrid speculatively.

Ingrid shrugged, still trying to appear nonchalant, but she knew she wasn't succeeding. "I like the city, you know that. But I can't see myself living there forever. I'd suffocate."

Shifting in her chair, Laura leaned forward. "How do you know what you don't like? You've lived in Springland all your life, but that doesn't mean you have to stay here forever."

"Laura, I'm surprised at you."

"Listen, Ingrid, men like Joel Stires are not easy to come by, and if you love him and want him, you'd better reach out of that snug little world of yours and grab him."

Ingrid blinked, surprised by Laura's attitude. She was sure Laura would have been the first one to object. "What are you saying?"

"I'm saying that somewhere along the line you've lost sight of your goals. I can remember when we were in high school all you dreamed of or talked of was traveling. You wanted to see all of the art treasures of the world. In fact, at one point, you figured out it would take you ninety-seven years to see everything you wanted to see and a hundred million dollars."

"Oh," Ingrid said, "I remember that. But that was just kids' stuff."

"Yes and no," Laura said brusquely, "but there's no reason why you can't start your dream in New York, where they have countless exhibits and an international airport."

"You're teasing me."

"Oh, no, I'm not. You're a free woman, Ingrid Christian. You're not shackled to Springland, Ohio. There's a whole world out there you've never explored." She gave her a wink. "Maybe Joel could explore it with you."

"I don't think he's very interested in art."

"What's keeping you from teaching him?"

"His bullheaded obstinacy, for one."

"You can manage that." Laura dismissed the issue with a quick flick of her wrist. "Men are very malleable, you know, once you learn how to work them."

Ingrid laughed, and then the bell rang and they both rose. Laura, leaning her head toward Ingrid, lowered her voice and spoke out of the side of her mouth. "Don't forget to keep me posted. I don't want to miss a single thing."

"Don't worry," Ingrid whispered back. "I'll take notes for you."

Ingrid's last class ended at four-thirty, and she decided to stop by her mother's house on the way home to drop off her croissant pan and, not incidentally, try to determine what her parents thought of Joel. Though she'd never let their opinions sway her one way or the other, she was still sensitive to their feelings. Besides,

Ingrid knew they liked him, and she wanted to hear all the good things they had to say.

Gussie greeted her at the door and, picking her up, Ingrid went into the glassed-in sun porch, where her mother was curled up in the corner of her favorite couch, knitting.

"I've been expecting you." She greeted Ingrid jovially. "And I even know why you came."

"To return your pan."

"To talk about Joel Stires." Mrs. Fenton patted the seat next to her. "Take your coat off and sit down and I'll give it to you straight." Her eyes sparkled with the teasing glint Ingrid knew so well. "To begin with," she began as Ingrid took the seat beside her and helped herself from the bowl of cashews, "your dad would adopt him tomorrow if he could. He thinks he's the most brilliant man to ever set foot in Springland, Ohio."

Ingrid laughed. "That sounds like dad. He's always been impressed with education."

"And success," her mother reminded her. "Like most men, he thinks prosperity is the ultimate goal."

"And what do you think?" Ingrid asked.

Her mother sighed wistfully. "I think he's devilishly handsome, brilliant, dashing, but maybe just a little tiny bit unscrupulous?"

Ingrid sat straight up. "What do you mean?" she demanded defensively.

"Now, cool down, honey, I didn't mean it the way it sounded." Mrs. Fenton focused her eyes on some distant point for a long moment. "What I'm trying to say is that, in his business, one would almost have to be a little unprincipled to survive."

"I don't understand."

"Yes you do," she insisted. "You just don't want to give it a hard look. By necessity, Joel has to do things, say things, treat people, whatever, in a way that will work to his advantage."

"But that's only in the courtroom," Ingrid argued. "And it's his duty to do whatever he can, regardless of whether it's unconventional or not, to get his client a fair trial."

Her mother looked at her pensively, then gave her hand a loving pat. "I suppose you're right," she conceded. "After all, if you're going to hire a famous criminal lawyer to defend you, you'd expect him to take advantage of every loophole to win your case."

Ingrid relaxed a little. "I know that's what I would expect. So he has to put on his little show now and then. That's better than letting an innocent person go to jail."

"You're right, dear." Her mother patted a wayward strand of hair in place. "I guess I'm just not tuned into the world of crime. But I want you to know that I think he's very charming and handsome."

Ingrid smiled. "I think he's very charming and handsome, too," was all she said.

"Oh, dear." Her mother sighed as she picked up her needles again. "Why couldn't I have had a daughter as talkative as Laura Moggs?"

"Because she'd drive you crazy, that's why," Ingrid

teased. "As much as you hate to admit it, you like the silent type. That's why you married Dad."

Mrs. Fenton sighed resignedly. "I know. He keeps telling me the only reason I married him was so I could do all the talking."

Ingrid laughed. "Just tell him he married you so he wouldn't have to open his mouth if he didn't feel like it."

Her mother's eyes lit right up. "You know, I never thought of that. Humph, the next time . . ."

As her mother went on with her dubious threats, Ingrid listened with only half an ear. Already her thoughts had drifted to Joel, and she wondered what he was doing and when he'd call. Because she was anxious to get back home in case the phone rang, she didn't stay long at her mother's. But as they said good-bye and Ingrid backed her car out of the driveway, the word *unscrupulous* lingered in her mind. Her mother was very perceptive. Did she sense something Ingrid had missed? No, no, of course not.

When she got home, Ingrid put the car away, changed clothes, fixed herself dinner, watched TV and worked on class assignments for the upcoming week. Then she waited and listened and fretted and finally, she worried. By eleven o'clock Joel still hadn't called.

Heartsick with anxiety, Ingrid turned in at eleven-thirty. Just as she switched out the light, the phone rang. Almost instantly all of the fretting she'd done in the past hour twisted into irritation. This was a hell of an hour to call.

"Ingrid? Joel," was the crisp voice.

"I thought it was King Kong."

There was a slight pause. "I won't keep you long since I can see you're not in your usual good humor. Just thought I'd tell you I got here."

"Oh, I'm glad you called, you know that," she said, relieved. "I was worried, that's all."

"No need to be. We worked until late and then went out to dinner at Carmichael's club and then sat around talking to some other lawyers for a while. I just got home."

"Oh, I see." Ingrid felt a slight twinge of resentment. While she'd been moping around all evening agonizing over why he hadn't called, he'd been out with the boys. But she forced herself to overlook it. He'd called, hadn't he? What more did she want?

"Oh, that's all right," she said. "I wasn't asleep. How did it go today?"

"Horrendously. Carmichael is running in circles. He has his finger in so many cases he can't remember who's a witness for whom. We finally got it all straightened out, though."

"No wonder he needed you in such a hurry."

"He needs two of me plus four assistants."

"I hope you won't let him run you into the ground."

"Don't worry, I won't," he assured her. "Now, how was your day?"

"Fine, but I missed you," she said softly and waited for him to say he missed her, too.

"Well, it won't be long. I have some depositions to

take tomorrow and the next day, but I should be able to get away Friday as planned."

"Sounds great." Was she a plan, now? A memo on his agenda? "Do you want me to meet you?"

"No, I'll fly into Cleveland and rent a car. I don't know what my schedule will be yet, but I'm expecting to be there by late afternoon or early evening."

"I'll keep a light in the window and the door unlocked."

"Good idea. I'll call you tomorrow if I can, but if you don't hear from me, I'll be there Friday."

They talked a few minutes longer before saying good night. Joel hung up first and when Ingrid heard the click and the dial tone, she just sat there and stared at the receiver in her hand. She had to blink to remind herself that the man she had just talked to was the same one who had held her in his arms in this very bed not twenty-four hours earlier. His voice had sounded stilted and hurried, as though he'd called because he'd felt obligated to, not because he'd wanted to enjoy a pleasurable windup to a long and harried day. But then, she reasoned, she hadn't been bubbling over with enthusiasm herself. Maybe it was just the hour and the anxiety of waiting and the fear that he wouldn't call.

Turning out the light, she slid under the sheets and pulled the covers up to her neck. Fear, she thought. Had she honestly thought he might not call? But that was absurd, she scolded herself. Of course he'd call. Whatever made her think otherwise? He'd promised he would and he did, just as she'd have done if she had promised to call him. The only difference was, she suddenly realized that she couldn't call him if she wanted to. She didn't have his number, she didn't know where he lived. If she had to get in touch with him, she'd have to contact Stanley Carmichael. And something told her that she and Stanley would not hit it off.

The morning brought with it sunshine and the promise of a beautiful day. Ingrid's restlessness of the night before was put on a back shelf, and by the time she was ready for school, she was in her usual good spirits. Turning on the car radio, she hummed along to the pop music. At school she talked to Laura and Peter, attended an art advancement program and inventoried supplies. But even though she was busy, the day dragged, and the evening was even worse. Joel didn't call at all, nor did he call the next day. Ingrid's mind whirled with conflicting emotions. On one hand, she was plagued by the worry that Joel had reverted back to the growling stranger she'd met at the airport and on the other, her spirits were buoyed up by the hope that he was still the same man she knew and loved.

On Friday, her last class ended at two. Ingrid dallied a little before leaving, stopping along the way for groceries, not wanting to get home too soon and spend the rest of the day waiting. But, to her amazement, a car was parked in her drive when she pulled in. Almost immediately, Joel burst out of the house—no boots, jacket wide open—and ran toward her with arms outstretched. With a whoop of delight, Ingrid fell into his embrace and clung to him as tightly as she could.

Clasping his arms around her, he lifted her right off

her feet. "Oh, God, Ingrid, you'll never know how good you look to me. I've been thinking of nothing but you all day."

"Me, too," she said, burying her head in his shoulder and closing her eyes. Her dreams had come true. He was here and he was the same Joel who had left her just days ago. Nothing had changed between them, nothing at all.

Finally Joel broke the embrace. "Come on, let's get these groceries into the house and put the cars away so we can spend the whole weekend completely free of responsibility."

"Sounds good to me."

Opening the car door, Joel reached inside and hauled out two heavy bags of groceries. "Here," he said, handing them to Ingrid. "You take these into the house, and I'll put the car in the barn."

Ingrid just stood still and grinned. Then, with a slight tip of her head, she turned and went into the house, Joel following with the groceries and complaining all the way. It was good to have him back.

Leaving the bags in the kitchen, they went back outside together, Joel's arm across Ingrid's shoulders, hers clenched tightly around his waist. She laughed up at him, blissfully happy, fully alive, her senses spinning with excitement. Even now her response to him was so powerful that she could feel a delicious shiver tremble through her veins. She hated to let go of him even for the few minutes it took to get the cars in the barn and slide the door closed behind them.

As they started back to the house, Joel put his arm

around her again and hugged her to him. "One of these days, I'd like you to explain to me why the cars are in the barn and the feed is in the garage."

"Well," she mused thoughtfully, looking down at the ground, "there really isn't any particular reason." Suddenly Ingrid stopped dead, the words frozen on her lips. "Uh-ohh," she said. "We'd better get in the house. Hurry."

"What's the matter?" Joel asked, startled.

Grabbing his arm, Ingrid tried to run, but Joel balked. "Come on, hurry," she urged.

"I don't see anyone."

"There are tracks in the snow." But the words were no sooner out of her mouth when she stopped dead. "Freeze!" she hissed under her breath.

Sensing the alarm in her voice, Joel stood motionless beside her and followed her eyes to the corner of the barn, where two big, bushy skunks stared back at them.

"Oh, my God," he murmured under his breath.

"Sssh!"

They stood like two stone statues watching, waiting, praying that the uninvited guests would leave quickly and cleanly. Sniffing the air, their noses quivering with suspicion, the skunks eyed their adversaries with a decidedly unpleasant look. For a full five minutes the skunks stood still, undecided, while Ingrid and Joel remained motionless, fingers crossed. The skunks, gradually realizing these two people were probably not out to harm them, proceeded slowly across the drive to the other side of the barn. At the corner, however, they paused to communicate with each other. Then one of them scurried around the barn out of sight while the other remained, pinning his antagonists with an evil stare.

"What do they want?" Joel whispered.

"Food. Sssh."

He waited another moment. "Don't they hibernate?"

"Only for six weeks at a time."

"Hell."

He was about to add something else, but the skunk's tail flicked warningly. Ingrid held her breath, hoping to God Joel wouldn't move. She could feel his impatience, greenhorn that he was, and realized he probably had no idea how much havoc one little skunk could cause. Suddenly, without any warning, the skunk spun around and dashed out of sight behind the barn.

Grabbing Joel's arm, Ingrid shouted, "Run!"

This time there was no resistance, no argument. They both broke into a full run and, racing up the walk, almost fell through the door.

Joel slammed it and locked it behind him before leaning against the wall, weak with relief. "Does this happen often?" he asked, gasping for breath.

"Only when they're looking for food," she answered as she started taking off her coat. "That's why I keep the feed in the garage. They'd never dare to come this close to the house."

"Well, at least that answers one question," he said, "but it raises another. How are you going to get your car out of there tomorrow?"

"They'll be long gone by then. They never stay out long in this weather."

"God, I hope you're right."

Joel was still in awe of his narrow escape when, moments later, he went into the living room and collapsed on the couch. With eyes half closed, head back, arms flung out, he looked like a wounded general on the battlefield.

"Water," he gasped, the dying man's last request.

"With a little Scotch in it?"

"If you think it would help."

"Probably not."

"Well, put some in it anyway."

"Might be harmful in your distressed condition."

"Not if it has very little water and two cubes of ice."

"And I hold your head in my lap and pour it down your throat."

"Somebody has to do it," he reasoned and reaching out, grabbed her by the wrist as if reluctant to let her go if only for a few minutes. "I don't see how you can exist in this wilderness. I've been here an hour and my nerves are shattered already."

"It's survival of the fittest," she said as she tried to free her arm, but he wasn't ready to release her and, admittedly, she wasn't ready to be released. Suddenly Joel lifted himself up from his supine position, caught Ingrid at the waist with both hands and, pulling her to the couch, tumbled her on top of him. Then, laughing at her surprise, he squeezed her with one of those big bear hugs of his that always left her breathless. Relaxing in his arms, she buried her head in his shoulder and planted a moist, sensuous kiss on his neck.

"Hmmm, good to feel you again," he purred contentedly. "You don't know how I missed you."

"Oh, yes, I do," she whispered, wiggling her hips a little in a deliberately seductive movement. "You're not the only one around here with sexual desires, you know."

Joel lifted his head to get a better look at her. "Those words sound like music." He grinned and, tightening his arms, he did a bit of wiggling of his own. Ingrid, a little amazed at the intensity of her reaction, tried to roll off to one side, but Joel stopped that by planting two large, powerful hands on her buttocks. "Where do you think you're going?" He grinned devilishly.

"I'm just trying to give you some breathing room, but if you don't want it . . ." She let the words trail off as she slid her hand to his waist and curved her fingers under the waistband of his pants. She could feel the quickening of his breath, as shifting slightly, she tunneled her fingers beneath the band and splayed them across the taut muscles of his stomach. Then, teasingly, instead of continuing downward and reaching lower, as she knew he anticipated, she clutched his shirttail and pulled it out of his pants.

"Ingrid . . ." he grumbled warningly.

"Joel . . ." she answered in the same tone. Reaching under his shirt, she ran her hand across his rib cage and upward to the coarse, dark hair on his chest. Pressing her palm into his skin, she began a slow, deep massage of his pectoral muscles. It was a silent dare, one Joel was quick to respond to.

"Mmmm," he murmured as his body, like hers, began to quiver with the hot flush of exquisite wanting. "Let's get out of these clothes."

Raising herself on one elbow, Ingrid began unbuttoning his shirt. Her movements were deft and sure, but slow.

"Hurry up," Joel urged, pulling at the tie of her blouse. "We can lie right here on the rug in front of the window and watch the sunset."

As Ingrid brushed a kiss across his cheek, her dark hair fell forward over his face. Teasingly, she shook her head. "I don't know how to tell you this, but the sun sets on the other side of the house."

Pulling her skirt up to her waist, he patted her on the buttocks. "That's even better. We'll stay and watch it rise." Then laughing, he clasped her around the waist and slid to the floor, pulling her with him. When she started to protest, he circled her neck with his arms and brought her lips to his.

The vibrant sensations that coursed through her at the touch of his mouth made Ingrid realize that her desire for him overrode everything else. Secure in the warmth of his embrace, the tormenting worries of the past week disappeared like the setting sun; in its place was the rosy glow of anticipation. Closing her eyes, she hugged him closer and allowed the longing ache within her to find the path to fulfillment.

Almost without realizing it, Ingrid found herself on the floor, disposing of her clothes with wild abandon.

The neat suit she'd worn to school was tossed aside with Joel's shirt and trousers. Her blouse was gone and she was taking off her panties and hose as Joel divested himself of his shorts. Then, grabbing the afghan from the back of the couch, he wrapped it around both of them and rolled them into a cocoon of warmth and happiness.

"You forgot the bra," he whispered huskily.

"I thought I'd leave that for you. You seem to do quite well with bras."

"Especially when they interfere with my total possession of a beautiful body."

Taking his time, he smoothed a hand down her hot skin and explored her hips and thighs before his fingers unhooked her lacy bra and sensuously pulled it away from her body. With a wanton sigh of pleasure, he cupped her breasts in his hands. Once again he sought her lips and smothered them with fiery intensity. Parting her lips, Ingrid welcomed the hot spear of his tongue as it moved across hers, massaging it, teasing it, prodding it with a gentle insistence that sent a shudder of ecstasy flooding through her.

Curling her into the curve of his body, he tightened the afghan around them and explored the soft ivory of her flesh while she slid her arms around him and explored the muscles of his back and shoulders. Lowering his head, he traced a line from her mouth to the swell of her breast and captured her nipple with tantalizing possessiveness. Ingrid's body trembled as shafts of delectable sensations coursed through her stomach and into her legs. Inhaling deeply, she gave herself completely to the rush of wild passion flooding through her.

"You're stirring up all kinds of arousals," she whispered hoarsely.

Ingrid felt his body shift and then his breath on her neck, hot and moist. "I have a few of my own that are straining to be set free," he said, his words muffled against her skin.

Sensuously, he pressed even closer into her burning flesh, and for many long moments they remained motionless, clinging to each other in the fading light, their senses taut with yearning. Then, slowly, their bodies began to move together until the arousal they had created reached the point of sheer agony. Burrowing her fingers deep into Joel's hair, Ingrid began to feel the powerful spiral of desire that had been building within her grow and swell and mount and soar until suddenly a violent tremor raced through her. She was conscious of nothing but the moist heat of her body and the soft moan that had escaped her lips.

"Let go," Joel whispered. "Let go."

"Come to me," she murmured back.

With a muffled cry of passion, he slid her slim body beneath his. Ingrid could feel the blood surging through him as the torrent of emotions they had both held in check began to swirl upward, dizzily out of control. With a gasp, he clasped his arms about her and drove into the depths of her flaming need. Instinctively, she arched into him; her body, understanding his rhythm, joined his. At first they swayed and glided then throbbed and surged until finally, with a force that left her gasping, a shock of burning rapture burst deep inside them both. Her body stiffened, trembled violently and drifted to someplace in heaven where there was only herself and Joel and the rosy twilight. She felt Joel caress her shoulder with gentle strokes, smooth the damp hair away from her face and kiss her forehead. Then the cocoon of warmth was tucked around her again and he was beside her and holding her and whispering softly.

"I love you, Ingrid."

Her eyelids fluttered open and she smiled into his eyes. "And I love you, too, Joel."

Together they burrowed into the drowsy warmth of one another. They were as one. How could she have ever imagined that anything could come between them?

Chapter Eleven

The following day, Stanley Carmichael called not once but three times, and each time, Ingrid overheard parts of Joel's end of the conversation. At first he was stern to the point of being rude, but as Carmichael poured out the atrocities their clients had to suffer, Joel listened more and more intently. Soon he was asking questions, giving advice and firing off a few condemning remarks of his own. Ingrid tried not to let this upset her, telling herself over and over that he was a famous criminal lawyer, that his work was not only vitally important but gratifying as well. Besides, every case took him closer to the top and that's where he wanted to go. He was an achiever; she'd known that from the beginning.

Sometime during the night, Ingrid had awakened to the realization that if she intended to travel the path to success with him, she'd have to make a lot of concessions. To her surprise, she found that she had reached a point where she was willing to do that. Though they were still getting to know each other's moods, the thread of understanding and love was weaving them closer together every day. Knowing that, she also knew that, somehow, they would manage to work around the rough spots and find the closeness they both sought so eagerly.

Admittedly, she felt a pang of jealousy at Carmichael's compelling influence over Joel, and even worried that Carmichael would entice him into something beyond his depth, but almost immediately she discarded that possibility. Joel was too clever for that. In fact, it wouldn't surprise her one bit if the day came when Joel shook himself free of Carmichael and opened his own office. But that would be years from now.

"Do you think the cop is lying?" Joel asked angrily, then listened in silence to the response. "We could trap him easily enough unless his partner's in on it, too." There was more silence and more conversation, but Ingrid deliberately tuned it out of her mind. It was none of her business. She'd do well to get busy and work up the exam for Wednesday instead of sitting around agonizing over Joel's problems. There wasn't anything she could do about them anyway. After all, she wasn't the lawyer; he was.

She wasn't surprised, then, when Joel came up behind her and put his arms around her neck, laying his cheek next to hers. "I'm afraid I have to leave tomorrow instead of Monday," he announced somberly. "I'm needed in California on Monday morning, but," he blew a kiss in her ear, "I'll be back by the middle of the week. I'm meeting Carmichael in Cleveland, and we're going to put some polish on the Canelli case."

Ingrid had never been one to suffer in silence. "Leaving!" she wailed. "But you just got here yesterday! We were going to spend the whole weekend together." She gave Joel a gentle push. "Go call him back and tell him to stuff it in his ear."

"I'd like to, but . . ."

"He doesn't own you. Remind him of that. And while you're at it, tell him that you're the mastermind of that firm, not him. Without you they'd be back writing wills for little old ladies."

"Right. Fire a shot across the bow. Threaten to quit."

"Tell him you want paid vacations and all holidays, legal or otherwise, off."

"And a Mercedes and my own private jet and an unlimited expense account."

"And four more assistants and a secretary to travel with you to handle all the mundane business matters."

Joel's brows rose with amusement. "You wouldn't mind if I had a good-looking secretary traveling around the country with me?"

"Of course not," she retorted. "As long as he's competent and efficient, who cares what he looks like?"

Taking a strand of her hair, he tugged gently. "Leave it to you to see the practical side of the situation," he said and, leaning closer, tormented the **V** of her blouse with his fingers. "Do you have to grade those papers now?" He not only put all the charisma he owned into the sensuous invitation, but supplemented it by dropping his hand a little lower.

Ingrid made no pretense at remaining unaffected. Placing her papers on the couch beside her, she raised her hands over her head and clasped them behind his neck, pulling him closer. "What did you have in mind?" she asked, her voice as seductive as his.

Leaving at noon the next day, Joel caught a plane from Cleveland to Los Angeles where, allegedly, he was needed to protect his client from the jaws of injustice, but there were times when he wondered if it wasn't the other way around. Jalara was typical of a lot of clients Carmichael and Brenhoun were getting lately: wealthy, spoiled, hotheaded, quick to expect absolution and willing to pay for lawyers like Joel to do the fighting for them. Often they refused to testify, which put even more of a burden on their attorneys. But so far, Joel had done well, especially in California, where a good performance was greatly appreciated.

It was here that Joel had gotten his basic training by carefully observing hyperreactional defense attorneys dramatically describe the torment their clients were going through because groundless charges had been filed against them. At first, Joel could hardly keep from laughing, but when he found out how effective these acts were, he changed his mind. The first time he tried his hand at a bit of theatrics, he felt ridiculous. But to his amazement, no one had paid any attention to him.

So he elaborated a little on the act, gestured more grandly, talked louder and more eloquently, utilized the power of the dramatic pause. Eventually he was not only noticed but appreciated.

To his credit, Joel prided himself on knowing his script well. He never went into the courtroom unprepared. There wasn't one quirk in the criminal law code that he didn't know and use. Joel was not only flamboyant and clever but brilliant, too, and *that* was where he had the edge.

He sighed, as he leaned back in his seat and stared out at the clouds below. Despite his name and fame, he didn't feel as if he'd reached his goal. He felt dissatisfied, fretful, hypertense. This wasn't like the self-confident Joel Stires, attorney extraordinaire from New York City. He knew, of course, what was causing his discontent. It was having to leave his dark-haired Ingrid standing in the driveway, waving good-bye. He wished to hell he could get off the stage, if only for a little while.

As Joel mulled this over in his mind, he came to the conclusion that what he really needed was a vacation. Maybe Ingrid and he could go someplace together. Atlanta would be nice. Besides, there was a wife-abuse suit coming up there next month. Maybe Ingrid would like to sit in on it. It held all the promise of a really gutsy ripsnorter. The defendant was accused of putting cyanide in the sugar bowl.

Ingrid hated to see Joel leave again, but she realized his presence in California was vitally important to his client. If it weren't for dedicated lawyers like him, a lot of innocent people would be found guilty and locked up for years. Still, she missed him terribly, especially when she filled the bird-feeding stations alone. But the knowledge that their separation would only be for a few days kept her going. Joel had already made his plane reservations back to Cleveland on Wednesday. That was just three days away and, though she felt empty without him, she knew she'd have to get used to his traveling. But then, she said to herself, he was worth the wait.

Joel called early Wednesday evening and, as before, his voice was clipped and sharp-edged, but this time Ingrid didn't mind it. She was beginning to realize that he was one of those people who sounded gruff over the phone no matter what they said or how they said it.

"Carmichael is here," he said, "and we're both going to see Borgas Canelli tomorrow. Then we have some witnesses to talk to, but we should be through by Friday noon."

"Then you'll be coming down here around two?" Another glorious weekend together, she thought.

There was a slight pause. "I'm sorry, Ingrid, but I don't think I can make it."

Her pulse gave a sudden, sickening thump, as if a claw of icy fear had suddenly gripped her heart. "Oh?" she managed.

"So why don't you come up here?"

She almost collapsed with relief, but her throat was still tight and though she tried to sound reasonably calm, she knew her voice was quaking with anxiety. "I suppose I could manage that without any trouble. Are you sure you want me?"

The answer was quick. "Of course I do. I wouldn't have asked you if I didn't. Now," he said in an oddly matter-of-fact tone, "can you meet me at the Sequoia Hotel on Cedarlane and East Fourteenth?"

"I know where it is."

"Good. We'll go out to dinner and to a show or something." Then, lowering his voice, he added meaningfully, "Don't forget to bring your overnight bag."

She could feel excitement churning in the pit of her stomach. He hadn't changed at all. Her imagination had been working overtime again. Would she ever learn?

On Friday Ingrid left directly from school. She'd managed to change clothes in the teachers' lounge without encountering the inquisitive Laura and had hurried out to the car before she was intercepted by a student. The roads were clear, the sun was out, the air had warmed considerably and her spirits soared with happiness. She didn't even mind the heavy freeway traffic or the slow, bumper-to-bumper progress through downtown Cleveland. All she could think of was Joel and the weekend that lay ahead of them. Though he hadn't said so, she assumed he'd be going back to New York on Sunday; strangely, she didn't even mind that. She'd come to accept a lot of things in the past few weeks and being separated from Joel from time to time was one of them.

Leaving her car with the parking-lot attendant, Ingrid went into the lobby. She was slightly disappointed that Joel wasn't there waiting for her with outstretched arms, but she knew that was ridiculous. He hadn't known her time of arrival any more than she had.

As Ingrid walked to the information desk, she was only vaguely aware of the appreciative glances of passersby. She was wearing what she called one of her 'big-city' outfits. She felt and looked tall and regal in her high heels, her pencil-thin black skirt and her tourmaline mink jacket. Her black hair was, as always, combed back away from her face, falling in shiny, thick folds on her shoulders. The lights from the chandeliers caught the shine in her hair as well as the glow in her eyes, revealing an inner happiness that was impossible to overlook.

Giving her name to the clerk, she asked him to ring Joel's room. When there was no answer, Ingrid looked puzzled. "Perhaps he left a message," she suggested.

Dutifully, the clerk looked in Joel's mailbox. He pulled out a desk memo and read the name on the front. "Ingrid Christian?" he asked and when she nodded, he handed it to her and turned his attention to another guest. As Ingrid opened the note, she was a little disappointed that it wasn't a personal one, something like "Glad you're here," scrawled in Joel's handwriting. The message was typed on plain white paper and simply stated that Mr. Stires would be in Conference Room 203A and would she meet him there? This undoubtedly, was the work of an efficient secretary.

As Ingrid walked across the lobby to the elevators, she felt vaguely nervous. She struggled with the disappointment she felt that Joel wasn't immediately free.

She hated the thought of interrupting a business meeting, feeling like an unwelcome intruder. But Joel *was* expecting her, wasn't he? Surely he'd have the week's business affairs wound up by now.

Ingrid got out of the elevator on the second floor and started looking for Conference Room 203A. She was glad she'd left her overnight bag in the car. She'd thought of bringing it but had changed her mind at the last minute. This was not exactly the way she'd visualized their meeting, but she shouldn't be childish about it, she scolded herself. Business was business, and, unfortunately, men had a tendency to put it before all else.

She found Room 203A without any trouble and knocked on the door.

"Who is it?" boomed a man's voice from within. It wasn't Joel, so it was probably Stanley Carmichael.

"It's Ingrid," she answered, trying to raise her voice without attracting attention.

"Who?"

"Ingrid," she repeated a little testily. Who in hell did he think it was, anyway?

She heard an answering murmur, then the sound of the night chain and, finally, the door opened. A tall, semigray-haired man in his early fifties stood there peering at her through the lower half of his bifocals. He was a nice-looking man in a rough sort of way, a little overweight and pompous-looking, and he reminded Ingrid of a toad. Though he pasted a smile on his face as soon as he saw Ingrid, she immediately sensed an underlying note of hostility in his attitude, as if her arrival had come at the worst possible moment.

"You must be looking for Joel. He went downstairs for a minute. He'll be right back." The smile widened a little as he held out his hand. "Stanley Carmichael."

"Ingrid Christian," she announced, her voice gracious but politely formal. As she'd known all along she would, Ingrid disliked Stanley Carmichael immediately. There was something oily-smooth about him that rubbed against the grain. He was also playing games, keeping her standing in the hall as long as possible. Was he trying to impress upon her that she was the servant and he the master?

Inwardly, Ingrid gritted her teeth, determined not to let Stanley Carmichael intimidate her, now or ever. After all, he was Joel's associate, the man he worked with every day, and she had no intention of causing friction between them. Besides, she reminded herself, she'd been wrong about first impressions before.

"Well! Come in, come in," Carmichael urged, as if suddenly remembering his manners and, standing aside, he let Ingrid pass into the room. She could feel his eyes following her every movement, taking in the details of her clothing, analyzing her walk, her carriage, her attitude. In short, he was sizing her up and, though it didn't bother her, Ingrid couldn't help but wonder why.

The room was large, with nondescript drapes pulled across the windows to keep out the sun. Its furnishings consisted almost entirely of one long conference table surrounded by mannish leather chairs. It was obvious that a meeting had just recently adjourned. Empty glasses, half-filled ashtrays, papers, legal forms, a tape recorder and two opened briefcases littered the table.

Ingrid paused a moment, half expecting Carmichael to pull out a chair for her. When he didn't, she sat down on one of the conference chairs, crossed her legs and shrugged out of her fur jacket. The upper portion of her sleek black outfit had a deep, square neckline that emphasized the graceful curve of her neck and complimented the pendant she was wearing, an exquisite emerald lavaliere surrounded by a circle of diamonds. Ingrid had hesitated wearing it, but was glad now that she had. If Carmichael thought Ohioans wore jeans and plaid shirts all the time, he'd underestimated them.

"Would you like a drink?" Carmichael asked suddenly, as though stirring himself from a reverie.

"No, thank you," she answered brightly. "We're going out to dinner later. I'll have one then. By the way, where is Joel?"

He shrugged evasively. "He should be back in a moment. We're all through here for today. At least Joel is. I still have another interview this evening."

Ingrid heard a key turn in the lock, and suddenly the door was flung open and Joel came striding into the room.

"Ingrid!" he cheered when he saw her and, arms outstretched, he closed the distance between them in two giant steps. As Ingrid jumped up to meet him, the gloom that had pervaded the room disappeared like magic. Joel's obvious delight at seeing her and the responsive thud of her heart and the heat in her cheeks left no doubt as to her feelings for this marvelous man she loved so much.

Wrapping his arms around her, Joel kissed her soundly on the lips. Ingrid knew he would have taken this a step farther if they'd been alone, but propriety prevailed. "Mmmm, you feel great," he said happily. Then standing back a little, he took a longer look at her. "My God, you look like a fashion model. Doesn't she?" he asked, turning to Carmichael.

The older man's response was a brief nod that Joel managed to ignore. Evidently Joel wasn't too impressed with Carmichael's less-than-perfect disposition either, Ingrid thought and wondered how Joel could stand to work with such an unpleasant person day in and day out. No wonder he was so restless all the time.

"Well," Joel said with a slap of his hands, "are we ready to go?" Then turning to Ingrid, he asked, "Where have you been anyway? I've been down in the lobby waiting for you."

"We must have just missed each other," she said, trying to hide her annoyance. Why hadn't Carmichael told her where he was? She'd have gone back down to get him. She slid Carmichael a hard, reproving glance, but he cleverly avoided it by pretending to be preoccupied with fitting his tape recorder into his briefcase.

While they watched, Carmichael packed and unpacked and fussed unnecessarily with his notebooks and pens as if stalling for time. When he finally got everything together, he turned to Joel. "We're going to have to replay all these tapes for the witnesses before they go on the stand. I noticed that Mrs. Smatherton said 'Wednesday' and the maintenance supervisor said 'Thursday.' Make sure they both understand they're to say 'Wednesday.'" He glanced up at Ingrid. "We don't want our witnesses fouling us up."

"Don't worry," Joel assured him. "I'll drill it into them before we get to court." He, too, began straightening his papers, stuffing some into his briefcase, handing some to Carmichael. They worked in silence for several minutes, then Joel paused and thought a moment. "I don't know how you feel about this, Stan, but I don't think we should put Canelli on the witness stand. I've told him a dozen times how to answer my questions, but he still can't remember what to say."

Carmichael stopped a moment to contemplate the suggestion. Then he nodded his head. "You know, you could be right. He *is* a little flaky. The prosecution could tear him to pieces, to say nothing of what the news media could do. Maybe we'd be better off just letting him sit at the defense table with a concerned look on his face. The cameras will be positioned to his left, so when he looks at the jury, he'll also be looking into the cameras, and he's very photogenic."

"And innocent-looking," Joel added. "We'll get lots of sympathy there."

"Right. As long as he keeps his mouth shut, we shouldn't have anything to worry about. God knows, we don't want him telling the jury anything that might backfire and send him to prison." Once again he glanced at Ingrid. "Bad for business."

Ingrid's eyes blinked open. Had she heard right? Did they actually think their client was guilty? Oh, no, she thought, they were just joking. Joel would never defend anyone who wasn't above suspicion. Carmichael might, she thought, but not Joel. Never. He'd become a criminal lawyer to defend the innocent, not free the guilty so they could go out and commit other crimes. Though Joel had admitted that the courtrooms of today were a stage and trials were battles between lawyers that everyone came to see, she knew he'd never do anything so unscrupulous as defend a man he knew was guilty. Unscrupulous? The word hovered around the edges of her mind. Had she heard it before in connection with Joel? No, no, it must have been someone else.

Finished with his packing, Carmichael snapped his briefcase shut. Suddenly he looked across the table at Ingrid. For a second, no more, his arrogant face froze as his piercing granite eyes locked with hers. Instantly Ingrid felt the cold tentacles of fear wrap around her. There was a message in those eyes, a menacing one. It was almost as if he were threatening her. Stiffening slightly, Ingrid shivered at this unknown dread. Then she shook herself sternly. She had nothing to fear from Carmichael. In fact, it could very well be the other way around. Not only was she a pretty good scrapper herself, but she had Joel on her side. And together they were an unbeatable team, anyone could see that.

Suddenly Carmichael's gaze shifted and the stony glare was suddenly replaced by an oily smile. "Well, I'll leave you two alone. It was nice meeting you, Ingrid."

With a nod, he picked up his briefcase and started for the door. "I'll see you in New York tomorrow, Joel," he added meaningfully, and left the room.

Joel stared at the closed door for a long moment, his mouth pressed into an angry line. Then, going to Ingrid, he put a hand on her shoulder. "I wanted to tell you myself, but he beat me to it."

"I was hoping we'd have the whole weekend together," she began, but her senses were so numb with disappointment and anger that she could hardly speak. The growing premonition that everything was going wrong hung over her like a black cloud, but she refused to give in to it.

"We'll have next weekend, I promise you." Joel's voice pleaded with her to understand, to be patient, to trust him.

And she did. Placing her hand on top of his, she rubbed it gently, then lifted it to her cheek, pressing it against her warm skin. "I realize how busy you are," she said quietly, "and I'm willing to take a backseat, but only temporarily." She glanced up at him. There was a flash of indulgent humor in the depths of her eyes. "However, I have my rights, too, you know."

Bending his head, he brushed a kiss across her half parted lips. "After this case, you'll not only have rights, but priorities. How does that sound?"

"It sounds great, but in the meantime," she teased, swinging her leg seductively, "what do you want me to do? Just sit here all evening and watch you work?"

"Not on your life. As soon as I get this stuff together, we're getting out of here." He finished gathering up the last of the notes and papers and shoved them into his briefcase. "Borgas Canelli can wait."

Ingrid felt a sudden stab of uneasiness at the mention of Canelli's name. Like "Carmichael," it was ominous, and she hated it. There had never been any shadows between her and Joel and she didn't want any, either. Not tonight, not ever.

Ingrid chose her words carefully, not wanting to sound accusing but at the same time getting right to the point. "From the way Carmichael talks, it sounds as if he thinks Borgas Canelli is guilty." She forced an off-handed, casual note into her voice. Her throat had tightened into a knot. Still, she pressed on; she had to know. "Is he?" she prodded.

Joel exhaled a patient sigh. "A man is innocent until he's proven guilty, you know that."

"You're not answering my question, Joel." Her voice was deadly serious.

"Who knows?" he said, unconcerned. "I've been hired to get him off, and that's what I intend to do."

"Regardless of the circumstances?" His evasive answer irritated her. Why couldn't he come right out and say what he thought?

She could see him struggling to keep his tone relatively civil. "Look, Ingrid, Canelli's wife is dead. Nothing can bring her back. What the hell difference does it make who did what?"

Suddenly she got to her feet and stared straight at him. "But if he's guilty, he should pay the penalty. Anything less is a miscarriage of justice."

He slammed the papers down on the table. "You

seem to forget that I'm paid to keep the accused out of prison," Joel snapped. "If I refused to represent any client who I thought might, perhaps, be guilty, I'd still be pushing pencils in the public defender's office."

Ingrid jerked back a little, stunned. This wasn't her Joel talking; it was Stanley Carmichael. Wrenching her eyes away from him, she crossed her arms and paced to the end of the room and back, but it did little to quell the turmoil simmering within her. Suddenly she stopped and faced him squarely. His expression was rock hard and belligerent. "Let me get this straight," she began, trying to breathe evenly. "Are you saying that you're working your tail off like this to get a guilty man free?"

Joel snapped his briefcase closed. "He's not guilty until proven—"

"I don't want to hear that!" she declared, her anger rising dangerously. "How dare you talk down to me under the guise of righteousness."

"Righteousness!" Slamming both hands on the table, Joel leaned toward her, his eyes flashing with outrage. "It seems to me you're the one who's so full of righteousness. All I'm doing is the job I'm paid to do."

"And if representing a guilty man serves your best interests then to hell with justice, is that right? Is that what you think, Joel?" Her voice was rising hysterically, but she didn't care. She'd reached a point where it seemed that all of her nightmares had come true.

Joel straightened, his eyes icy cold, his voice icily polite. "Listen, Ingrid, you may find this hard to believe, but when I'm in that courtroom, I'm playing for very high stakes. And when I win a case, I have saved someone's life."

"If you're so interested in saving lives, then you should have become a doctor," she shot back. "Lawyers are supposed to fight for justice, not make a travesty of it."

"Justice!" he bellowed. "Do you really think a criminal trial is the epitome of justice? Well, let me tell you something. A criminal trial is a contest between competitors, and the prize is the life of the defendant. It's that simple."

"And what about the life of the victim? Didn't that have any value?"

"I don't know and I don't give a damn," he blazed, furious. "The victim is not my client and does not pay my fee."

"You're a mercenary bastard!"

Joel threw a pencil across the table. "Honest to God, Ingrid, I can't believe your naiveté. Obviously you've been too long in Pollyanna's art class."

Ingrid was so furious she couldn't even breathe. Never had anyone spoken to her like that, angered her like that, insulted her like that. Why, he was no better than Stanley Carmichael! Worse, in fact. At least with Carmichael she knew where she stood the moment she met him.

Biting her lip, she tried to block out the torment, but the anger hanging in the air between them was like an invisible dagger. She couldn't hold it in any longer.

With a sudden flash of defensive spirit, she snatched her coat from the chair, picked up her handbag and started for the door.

"Where do you think you're going?" he snarled.

"Back to Pollyanna's art class, where I belong," she flung over her shoulder, and slammed the door so hard it rattled the mirrors on the walls.

Chapter Twelve

*I*ngrid bypassed the elevator and took the stairs to the lobby, fighting desperately to control the rage within her as well as the tears of anger that stung her eyes. She paused before going into the lobby to put on her jacket. Then, wiping a telltale tear from her lower lashes, she took a deep breath, squared her shoulders and wove her way through the crowded lobby with the grace of a swan.

Pushing through the revolving doors, she gave her parking ticket to an attendant and waited out in the cold for her car. She was shivering by the time it arrived, but at least the air had calmed her wrath a little. It had been a long while since she'd lost her temper that way and, though she knew it was a childish thing to do, she also knew it couldn't have been avoided.

Getting into her car, she drove away from the hotel entrance with a composure that surprised her. As she wove through the Cleveland traffic toward the freeway entrance, however, she began shaking all over. Big, wet tears started brimming in her eyes, but she wiped them away quickly with the back of her hand and forced herself to concentrate on the road. It wasn't until she reached the south side of town and the traffic had thinned out a little that the enormity of the situation began to sink in. She had just walked away from the man she had loved so much that she thought nothing could ever come between them. He had been her knight in shining armor, her protector, her Lohengrin. *Oh, God,* she sobbed, what happened, what happened?

Many hours later, Ingrid sat huddled in the depths of an easy chair, watching the flickering shadows of the moon on the snow-covered field outside the window. The designer dress and the suede pumps and the glittering pendant had been replaced by the granny gown that Joel had admired once. The memories were so vivid, so close, that she let her thoughts run backward deliberately. Through it all, she knew that Joel had been right about one thing. She had been naive, as well as immature and foolish.

From the very beginning she had known their lifestyles ran in opposite directions, but she had waved aside the warning signals and convinced herself that if they were willing to make a few concessions on each side, all would be rosy and bright. If that had been the only stumbling block, it would have worked, but what she hadn't realized was that their values were as opposite as their backgrounds. Her mother had seen this and tried to warn her, but wisely she had backed off, knowing Ingrid would have to discover it for herself. Even Carmichael, in that repugnant, sinister way of his, had tried to scare her off. But Ingrid had blindly ignored the danger signs and had taken the ride to its crashing finale.

And that's what the argument between her and Joel had been—a finale. It was over between them, she knew that. She could never reconcile herself to his way of thinking, nor he to hers. They were like creatures from different planets.

Yet, in spite of everything, she still loved him. She was hopeful that time would ease the pain. It always did, didn't it? People picked up the pieces of their lives and went on. It happened every day. It had happened to her just over a year ago, and she'd managed, hadn't she?

Rising from her chair, she made herself stand up straight and tall. But the tears that had been trembling on her eyelids refused to stay confined any longer and rolled down her cheeks in long smears. Quickly, she brushed them aside and, swallowing tightly, crossed the room to the window to close the drapes. She paused a moment, her eyes lingering on the white slope of hill, the blue-tinged shadows of the trees, the moon, bright and unwinking in the cloudless sky.

Why was it that everywhere she looked she saw Joel walking toward her?

Joel was absolutely stunned when Ingrid slammed out of the conference room. He couldn't believe she'd do a thing like that . . . she was so levelheaded. He was sure, however, that she hadn't gone far, probably down to the bar to join Carmichael for a drink. And perhaps it was just as well. God knows, they needed a cooling-off period. It was hard to believe that anyone in America today still thought that all guilty defendants were punished and all innocent ones were set free. That theory was almost a joke nowadays. In fact, he hadn't heard it since he graduated from law school. Even when he was in the public defender's office, it was the fast-talking lawyer who won the case, not the testimony of the innocent. Surely Ingrid knew that.

Snapping his briefcase shut, Joel made sure he hadn't forgotten anything before he turned out the light and closed the door. As he walked down the hall and waited for the elevator, he kept trying to rationalize Ingrid's behavior, as well as his own. He realized *naive* was not the word he should have used. Ingrid was not only bright and witty and intelligent, but she was perceptive, too. Of course she was aware of the injustices of the judicial system. The problem was, she still clung to the theory that it was the duty of lawyers to screen clients to make sure they represented only the innocent ones, not those who were suspect. Joel had to admit that in most cases this wouldn't be hard to do, but it was so impractical.

As Joel stepped out of the elevator in the lobby, he looked around. When he didn't see Ingrid, he checked his briefcase at the main desk and went into the bar. Carmichael was sitting on a stool talking to the man next to him. He waved when he saw Joel and motioned to a table, indicating that he wanted to talk to him in private. Joel nodded, but he wasn't ready to sit down. His eyes scanned the dimly lit bar for Ingrid, and when he didn't see her, he went out into the lobby again and quickly looked around. Then he reentered the bar.

"Where's Ingrid?" he asked as he and Carmichael squeezed into a narrow booth and ordered drinks.

"Don't ask me," Carmichael said, shrugging. "Why? What happened? Did you two have a little argument?" His voice held a slight note of hope, Joel didn't find very amusing.

"Yes, as a matter of fact, we did, but nothing serious. I thought she was down here with you having a drink."

"Ingrid here with me?" Carmichael asked, lifting his brows in amazement. "I'm afraid this would be the last place on earth she'd be. She hates my guts."

"Oh, for God's sake, Stan, stop exaggerating, will you? She doesn't hate anybody's guts."

"You want to bet?" He raised his glass. "Loser buys."

"I bet on horses, not women," Joel growled, still looking around, expecting her to walk in any minute.

"Okay," Carmichael said, "have it your way, but I think you and your friend are going to have a few differences of opinion. Big differences, like the size of the Grand Canyon."

Joel listened with half an ear and sipped his drink. "Be specific, will you?"

"All right, if that's what you want." Carmichael took a long swallow and set his glass down. Then, leaning his elbows on the table, he clasped his hands together. Joel recognized this as his serious-business pose and a frown creased his brow. What was up, anyway?

"I think your friend Ingrid is very lovely, beautiful and charming. But she is also out of your world, Joel. She still believes in the tooth fairy."

"She believes in justice," Joel retorted in sudden defense of Ingrid.

"Sure, don't we all? But a few of us happen to know that our legal system is not exactly perfect and, if it weren't for criminal lawyers like us, there'd be thousands of innocent people behind bars right this minute."

"Yeah, I know that. I've heard it all before," Joel said impatiently as once again his eyes roamed over the heads of the people in the bar. "Where is she, anyway?"

"My guess is that she left for home."

Joel looked at him sharply. "Did you see her go?"

"No," he admitted, "but women like Ingrid don't stay around to slug out the battle to the bitter end. They prefer to remove themselves from the problem until they can get a better perspective." He drained his glass and signaled the bartender for another. "In other words, she's probably gone somewhere to sulk. But don't worry, she'll call you back tomorrow full of apologies."

Joel slid him a suspicious glance. "What makes you think you know so much about women?"

"I know a lot about people. Don't forget, that's my job. If you'll just sit back and do nothing and give Ingrid time to simmer down, she'll be in touch with you. Don't worry."

Joel went back to his room as soon as he and Carmichael left the bar and sat there all evening, waiting for Ingrid to call. He didn't leave his post for a minute for fear of missing her. He ordered sandwiches and coffee from room service, a far cry from the exquisite cuisine in the Crystal Room that he'd planned to enjoy with Ingrid. Finally he tore up the theater tickets and hauled out his briefcase. But even though he was behind in his work, he found it impossible to concentrate.

He looked around him. The room he'd looked forward to sharing with Ingrid seemed very large and terribly empty. He'd expected it to be filled with talk and laughter and the easy bantering they both loved so well; just as he'd expected to see her suitcase next to his, her filmy nightgown over the chair, her shoes kicked aside in hasty abandon. He could almost feel her body, warm and sweet-smelling, as they huddled together, their naked desire ready for fulfillment.

Twice he almost called her, but Carmichael's words of advice still rang in his ears. Besides, though he missed her, he was still angry with her. She'd thrown some pretty serious accusations at him that still rankled, and as much as he wanted to talk to her, he didn't want to risk starting the argument up all over again. A short cooling-off period was what they both needed. He could almost hear Ingrid telling herself to 'sleep on it' which, actually, wasn't bad advice. He'd do well to follow that advice himself. Besides, it was late, almost midnight. Joel knew Ingrid wouldn't call now. She'd wait until morning.

However, when Ingrid hadn't called by noon the next day, Joel decided to hell with cooling off, this had gone on far enough. He called her but there was no answer. He tried again an hour later; still no answer. Where in hell was she? He and Carmichael had to catch an afternoon flight to New York, and then there was a dinner and business meeting at the club. He wouldn't be able to call her again until he got back to his apartment, around ten or so.

Unfortunately, the party lasted longer than Joel had expected and rather than wake Ingrid up in the middle of the night, he decided to wait until morning. Tomorrow was Sunday. She'd be home, sitting at the table in the living room grading papers. A strand of dark hair would fall across her face, and she'd push it back impatiently and look across the table at him and smile. But this was ridiculous, Joel chided himself. He was seeing visions. And he didn't want to see them, he wanted to hold them.

Joel was sitting at his oversized desk in the plush offices of Carmichael and Brenhoun, dictating into a tape recorder, when Carmichael trounced in. He had the annoying habit of noisily interrupting the other lawyers in the office whenever a new idea popped into his head. Normally this didn't bother Joel at all, but lately he found it very irritating. It had been a week since he and Ingrid had parted in Cleveland. He'd tried to get hold of her for three days without success before he finally admitted she was deliberately avoiding his calls. The uneasiness he'd felt the first few days after the argument soon became a dull, tormenting ache that never left him. And Carmichael's nagging presence and probing questions only added to his wretchedness.

Carmichael, however appeared jubilant. "Say, I've just thought of a new slant on that Gorman case."

Joel didn't even look up. "Yeah? What is it?"

"Oh God," Carmichael said. "Are you still moping?"

"I'm trying to get some work done, Stan. What can I do for you?"

"Okay, okay, I get it," he said, throwing his hands up in the air. Still, he didn't remove himself from the office. Instead he hiked his hip up on the edge of Joel's desk and leaned toward him. "I sure as hell hope you snap out of this slump you're in before the Canelli trial comes up."

"I haven't failed you yet, have I?"

"No, but you haven't acted like this before, either. Just because you got your ego bent out of shape a little doesn't mean you have to go around looking like a sick dog, you know."

"Maybe my ego needed a little bending," Joel conceded.

"Nonsense. You and I have enormous egos," Carmichael observed, "but you have to remember that if we didn't have them, we wouldn't be where we are today. It's our egos that keep us going. We're like actors. We enjoy performing in the courtroom, we love to act out a whole range of emotions for the benefit of the jury. We like to impress the judge, confuse our opponents and provide the news media with lots of little surprises that they can blow up way out of proportion. Face it, Joel. We're a couple of hams, and we love it."

"The ham part I'll go along with. But love it?" Joel grimaced and shook his head. "I don't know about that."

Carmichael shot him a reproving glance. "Well, you'd better love it. It happens to be your bread and butter, in case you've forgotten." When all Joel did was shrug noncommittally, he pressed on. "What's the matter with you? Have you forgotten that you've been working your tail off for eleven years to get where you are today? Here you are, thirty-six years old and already you're a celebrity. And I'll tell you something else. When you win this Canelli case, you're going to be in the top ten." He eyed Joel closely. "I just hope to God you're not going to louse it up because some woman walked out on you."

"I'm not going to louse up anything!" Joel snapped irritably. Shoving his chair back, he stood up and jammed his hands in his pockets, then took a deep, calming breath. "I realize the importance of the Canelli case, Stan. To me, to you, to the whole office. But I am worried about our defending so many clients whose innocence is very questionable."

"Questionable!" Carmichael shouted. "So what? As

long as they don't confess, they're not guilty. Not in my book, not in anyone's book." He looked sharply at Joel. "Canelli didn't say anything to you, did he?"

"No, of course not. He's dumb, but not so dumb that he doesn't know we have to turn him in if he confesses to us. What I'm saying is," Joel went on, "the firm could be getting a bad name."

"How do you figure that?"

"Reason it out for yourself. When was the last time we had a client who was absolutely above suspicion? Someone we honestly felt was being prosecuted unfairly?"

"Oh God, Joel, get off it, will you?" Carmichael said. "Clients who can afford the kinds of fees we charge don't grow on trees, you know."

Joel's shoulders slumped slightly in a gesture of resignation. "I know. And you're right. But just the same, it'd be a nice change if just once I could sink my teeth into a case where my client was so obviously innocent that it would sock you in the eye."

"If he was all that innocent he probably wouldn't have been apprehended in the first place."

"Oh, yes, he would. It happens every day."

Carmichael sighed peevishly. "Well, what about the Jalara trial in California that's coming up? Is he innocent enough for you?"

"Huh!" Pressing his mouth into a flat line, Joel gave Carmichael a cynical smirk. "Come off it, Stan. Who do you think you're kidding?"

"So it's a little iffy," Carmichael admitted with a toss of his head. "So what else is new?" When Joel didn't respond, he gave him a long, hard look. Then, absently, he ran his hand through his graying hair, a habit he had when he was trying to reach a decision. Suddenly he looked up. "All right. I'll give that one to Cummings, but you're going to have to brief him."

Joel nodded, agreeing. "That shouldn't be too hard. He's pretty sharp."

"But not as sharp as you. Jalara isn't going to like this. He's expecting our star performer."

"Tell him your star performer is going to take a nice, long, well-deserved vacation as soon as the Canelli trial is over."

"Oh?" Carmichael's brows lifted ominously. "Are you trying to tell me something?"

"Yes, damn it," Joel retorted hotly. "I'm trying to tell you that I'm taking some time off before my head comes unscrewed."

"And where are you planning on spending this time off? In the woods with your girl friend?"

Joel's hackles rose straight up at Carmichael's sarcastic tone. Angrily, he kicked the chair under the desk. "Frankly, I'd like nothing better, but I doubt if I'd be welcomed with open arms. She'd probably turn her skunks loose on me."

"Skunks?"

"Forget it. It's just a joke."

"Then why aren't you laughing?"

Joel realized that, in his own way, Stan was trying to cheer him up. For the first time in almost a week, Joel's face broke into a smile. "Scram out of here, will you? I'm trying to get some work done."

Carmichael returned the smile, glad that things were getting back to normal. "I'm on my way," he promised and sallied out of the office, satisfied that his top man was once again securely under his thumb.

Joel watched him go. Carmichael hadn't changed much since he'd first met him seven or eight years before. Joel had been working in the public defender's office since graduating from law school and had won some tough cases. Carmichael, always on the lookout for a bright new lawyer to promote, had offered Joel an opportunity he couldn't turn down. It meant a lot of hard work, many long hours, much traveling, but the rewards were worth every ounce of effort he'd put into it. Today Joel was not only financially well off, but his name carried with it the ambience of success. His boldly handsome face and winning courtroom style had made his trials popular with the news media. And, he thought grimly, that was vitally important, wasn't it?

Sitting back down at his desk, he exhaled a long, weary sigh and picked up his pen again, but held it motionless in his hand. Reluctantly, he had to admit that he'd lost something along the way, too. Marilyn had left him before he'd even been with Carmichael a year, and almost all of the friends he'd had when he was in the public defender's office had drifted away to be replaced by new ones with keener minds and larger wallets.

Suddenly he got up again and went over to the window, pulling open the drapes. For many long minutes he stood watching the busy street below. People bustled in and out of stores, taxis wove their way through the traffic, buses stopped and disgorged passengers and loaded them back up again in the never-ending cycle of public transportation.

And then he raised his eyes to the building directly across the street from him, and then up farther to the rooftops.

It had started to snow.

He would always think of Ingrid when it snowed: her red cap, her big, round, brown eyes, her quick smile and easy laugh. He could almost see her now as he helped her carry the grain into the woods and stood and watched the fluid motions of her body as she filled the bird feeders and spread the hay and bent to coax a squirrel to eat out of her hand. She was a beautiful person, inside and out, and though he'd only known her a short while, he knew he'd been a privileged person.

Turning his back to the window, he glanced around his office, at the piles of papers on his desk. Why was it, he wondered, that some people, like Ingrid, could set their sights and follow the course unerringly?

He'd started out like that. Serving justice. That was what he'd championed all through law school. Even when he was a public defender, he'd firmly believed in the fundamental principle of justice. There had been no murky areas, then, no false values, no illusions of grandeur, just hard work and the frequent exhilaration of a victory well earned. Somewhere along the line, however, his goals seemed to have changed. But where? he wondered, and how?

Suddenly, the door to Joel's office burst open, startling him out of his reverie. It was Carmichael again. This time he was so excited he was almost dancing.

"You won't believe this," he said, striding up to Joel's desk and carefully smoothing out the sheet of memo paper he'd been carrying. "Just feast your eyes on that, my friend, and then try and tell me we aren't the greatest!"

For a moment Joel thought Carmichael was going to take flight. He'd seen him exuberant before, but never like this! The whole atmosphere of the room was so charged with electricity that even Joel's adrenaline started to soar. This was the part of law he liked, the thrill of something new and challenging at every corner.

"Well, come on, tell me, what is it?" Joel asked. He enjoyed Carmichael's clowning around. It always meant they'd hit the jackpot. Instantly Joel's senses started to throb with excitement.

"Sit down, chum, you're going to need a chair under you when you hear this." Dutifully, Joel did as told, trying hard not to let his eagerness show. It would ruin Carmichael's act, which began with a pompous stance and a theatrically serious expression. Finally he folded his arms across his chest and cleared his throat. He was ready. "One of the most eminent members of the House of Representatives has just been caught with a whole boatload of cocaine!"

"No!" Joel exclaimed. He couldn't believe it. "Who?"

Leaning across Joel's desk in his famous declarative pose, he spoke slowly, carefully spacing his words for the best dramatic effect. "Raymond J. Chesterton the Third, sole heir to the Falke Oil millions."

Joel's eyes widened with shock. "Oh, my God!" he swore. "I can't believe this. And he called us?"

"Not directly, but his family did. They want nothing but the best for their big daddy." He nudged Joel's arm. "And they made it very clear that cost was irrelevant. And I made it very clear that we didn't come cheap."

Joel could hardly believe what he was hearing. Raymond Chesterton was one of the most controversial figures in Congress. Rumors had it that he had bought his way in and intended to stay there. His son was running for governor of his state and his wife was on the society pages every week. She threw lavish parties, sponsoring benefits for everything from bicycle racing to art exhibits. They were both recognized on sight all over Washington and New York. This one would make the Canelli case look like peanuts, Joel thought.

"Well, come on," Joel urged, "fill me in. What in hell happened, anyway?"

"Allegedly," Carmichael rolled the word around on his tongue like a piece of candy that tasted so good he hated to swallow it. "*Allegedly,* he was trying to smuggle narcotics into New York harbor on his famous yacht, the *Sprinta.*"

"I don't believe it. Even Chesterton isn't that dumb."

"Wrong. Chesterton is that dumb," Carmichael corrected.

"What makes you think that? He didn't confess, did he?"

"No, thank God."

"Then what's his alibi?" Joel prodded. "He does have one, doesn't he?"

"I haven't questioned him, of course, but according to his wife, he swears someone put those narcotics on his boat without his knowledge for the sole purpose of damaging his political image. *Allegedly,* he didn't even know they were there until the authorities found them."

Joel stroked his chin thoughtfully. "It's entirely possible. What do you think?"

Carmichael came around the desk and slapped an all-knowing, reassuring hand on Joel's shoulder. "You forget, we're not paid to express our personal opinions, only those of our clients. Our job is to defend. Period."

"And how are we going to do that? Do we have to rely on his word as a patriotic statesman versus that of the authorities who arrested him?" It sounded like a good approach.

Carmichael, however, shook his head. " 'Fraid not. Unfortunately, he was arrested on a tip from three witnesses who swear they saw him help load the stuff onto the boat. But so what?" Carmichael slid him a cunning look. "We can get ten witnesses to swear he was at a party somewhere else. With his money, that should be as easy as pie."

Chapter Thirteen

Despite Ingrid's determination to be brave and face reality and forge onward in the face of disappointment and failure, she had trouble pumping her old enthusiasm back into her daily routine. After she and Joel had had their fight and she had come home alone to the empty house, she'd lain awake all night staring into the darkness, hoping the phone would ring, that he would be there on the other end to tell her she had misunderstood him, that his values were the same as hers and he would come down and explain it to her in person.

Ridiculous, wasn't it? she thought later. How foolish the heart can be, and how easily torn. Yet still, in spite of all that had happened, her feelings toward Joel were just as deep as they ever had been. It was something she could do nothing about. She'd just have to live with it, she decided, until time blurred his memory into the shadows of the past.

The next morning when she'd gotten up, she'd felt headachy and depressed and decided she'd better get hold of herself before she was carried away by self-pity. Dressing warmly for a day out-of-doors, she made herself eat breakfast before going outside. Though it had warmed up considerably in the past week, much of the wildlife winter food was still buried in snowdrifts. So Ingrid had hiked through the woods and checked the feeding stations. She'd tied three bales of hay onto a sled and tramped over a mile through deep snow dropping off half bales as she went. It wasn't hard work, but it was exhausting, and it provided a small measure of therapy.

When Ingrid had finished, she'd stopped back at the house only long enough to get her purse and her errand list before leaving again. She'd decided to go through the motions of her regular Saturday chores if it killed her. Languishing on the couch all day, reliving every angry word that had been exchanged, would only prolong the anguish. What she needed was a change of scenery. Yet when she'd gotten into the truck and backed it out, she could imagine Joel sitting next to her, watching the road, shouting orders, looking at her out of the corner of his eye as though testing her tolerance level. Odd how much she missed his teasing, almost as much as she missed his arms.

Stop it, Ingrid, she'd scolded herself as she wiped away a stray tear. She took a deep breath. Maybe she'd postpone the errands until that afternoon, she'd decided, and stop in and see her mother, who was always a great comfort when the days looked the darkest.

Mrs. Fenton was studying the complexities of a hand loom when her daughter entered. But she put it aside as soon as Ingrid sat down on the couch, put her head back and looked up at the ceiling. It was obvious she'd been crying and was trying her hardest to work herself out of a deep problem.

Sitting down beside her daughter, Mrs. Fenton also put her head back, sighed and stared up at the ceiling. For several minutes they sat there in companionable silence. "You and Joel had a fight," Mrs. Fenton had stated simply.

Ingrid nodded wordlessly.

"I take it, then, you're not speaking?"

"That's correct."

There was a moment's pause. "Are you not speaking to anyone or not speaking to Joel?"

"Oh, Mom, you know what I mean."

"Of course I do. I'm just trying to get you to talk. It always helps."

"I've been talking to myself all night."

"You must be bored with yourself by now." She'd patted Ingrid's hand. "Try me for a change."

Ingrid had nodded and cleared her throat and swallowed. Finally, haltingly, she'd explained what had happened between her and Joel. She didn't embellish the story nor did she leave anything out, starting with Carmichael opening the door for her and ending with her stormy exit, the long drive home, the sleeplessness, the frustration, the self-condemnation.

Her mother had listened in thoughtful silence, not speaking until Ingrid had talked herself out. Then she had taken Ingrid's hand between hers and held it tight.

"You know, Ingrid, you have a very strong sense of fairness. You always did. And I admire you for it. But you have to realize that not everyone shares your point of view."

"In other words, I'm naive."

"Stop beating yourself, will you, and listen?" Turning to face Ingrid, she had rested her arm across the back of the sofa. "I'm not just talking about Joel. Many people, especially those in big business, have had to resort to rather underhanded tactics to get ahead and stay ahead. The corporate ladder is a vicious climb and often requires actions that would never meet your strict standard of honor. They're jokingly referred to as bribes, payoffs, favors, hush money, payola—the list is endless."

Ingrid had turned to face her mother. "Are you trying to tell me I'm just too goody-goody for my own good?"

"No. The point I'm trying to make is that not everyone sees things as black and white as you do. To them, fudging a little here and there is good business practice."

"Hmm." Ingrid thought, then looked straight at her mother. "Do you think it's right for the life of the guilty to have preference over the life of the victim?"

"Of course I don't, but that's not what I'm saying," Mrs. Fenton had replied firmly. "You keep missing my point. What I'm trying to say is that some people do not think this is unscrupulous. They honestly believe they're doing the right thing."

"Do you think Joel feels that way?"

"I'm giving him the benefit of the doubt, and I think you should, too. I think he's been caught up in this big whirlwind of the reputation he has and hasn't really stopped to reassess his goals for a long time. And from what you tell me, I'd say Carmichael is largely responsible for it. He's kept Joel so busy that he hasn't had time to look around him."

"And he probably never will."

"Not if Carmichael can help it. Joel's his number-one boy, and he keeps him pumped up by telling him how great he is and how far he's going to go if he stays with him."

"And Joel believes every word of it," Ingrid had commented dryly.

"Don't be so hard on him, honey. Ego plays a big part in this, but there's something else, too."

"What's that?"

"Challenge. I think Joel is a very competitive person."

"Oh, is he ever! He even competes with himself."

"Exactly. Joel thoroughly enjoys the courtroom duel between himself and the prosecuting attorney. He's an achiever, and he's going to win at all costs."

"Even if winning means setting a guilty person free?"

Mrs. Fenton had shaken her head. "He doesn't see it

that way, Ingrid. At this point in his career winning is more important than how the game is played. And then?" She'd splayed her hands outward in a gesture of emptiness. "You come along and tell him that what he's been rewarded for all these years is really contemptible. Can you blame him for being confused?"

"I suppose not," Ingrid had admitted, "but it still doesn't make a wrong right."

"No, dear, but it does muddy the water. Joel's probably sitting in his hotel room right this minute trying to understand your feelings just as you're trying to understand his."

Ingrid shook her head. "Believe me, when we parted, there was no misunderstanding."

"That bad, huh?"

"That bad."

Mrs. Fenton had given her daughter an affectionate pat on the knee. "Your dad will be back in a few minutes. Why don't you go out and check the wells with him this afternoon? He'd love to have your company."

"You know?" Ingrid had said, "I just might do that."

"Good. And when you get back we'll have dinner. Would you like to spend the night? I'd love to have you."

The invitation was as welcome as one of Joel's big bear hugs. "That's the best suggestion I've heard all week."

Ingrid hadn't gotten home until late Sunday afternoon and had dallied around outside as long as she could before finally going in and facing the empty house. The next day had been Monday and though she had no classes, she'd decided to go to school anyway and spend some time working on the freshman class's spring exhibit. She had taken great care applying her makeup and had fussed with her hair for a half hour before it was just right. One thing she'd learned from the turmoils of the past was, if you feel bad, don't look bad.

Laura had been surprised to see her. "What's this? Working on your day off?"

"Well, if you'd call an exhibit work, I guess you could say that."

Jokingly, Laura had cast a glance past Ingrid's shoulder. "Where's your handsome guest? Did he go back so soon?"

"Well," Ingrid had hedged, "yes. He had a lot of work to do."

"I should think so, with that Borgas Canelli trial coming up, plus the seminar this weekend."

Ingrid blinked. "Seminar?"

"Yes, the seminar, remember? Seminar?" Laura had teased. "It was postponed because of the storm?"

"I remember all right." Would she ever forget?

"Well, it's finally been rescheduled for this Saturday. The notice is on the bulletin board right there." Just as she'd pointed, the bell rang. "Oops, I've got to go. See you at lunch?"

"Sure."

As soon as Laura had turned the corner at the end of the hall, Ingrid had gone over to the bulletin board. A large glossy placard announced the coming of the seminar that had been postponed. Ingrid hadn't read the particulars. Her eyes only saw Joel's picture in the center of the poster. He looked very professional and dedicated and handsome, a compelling person, one you wouldn't want to miss. But to Ingrid, it wasn't the Joel she knew. There was no glint of amusement in his eyes, his brows weren't lifted inquiringly, his mouth wasn't as full and soft as she remembered. Yet as she stood there, she could still feel his massive shoulders, his broad hands on her back, his breath on her cheek, the crushing warmth of his strength. Ingrid had quickly caught herself and looked around hastily to see if anyone had been watching. The hall was empty. Her secret was safe, but her heart was in her throat.

Ingrid couldn't help but wonder if Joel would come out to see her or call her or talk to her. But perhaps he was still bitter over her accusations and never wanted to set eyes on her again. God knows, he hadn't called or made any move to contact her, but maybe that was just as well. Why be tormented with fresh wounds? They were traveling in different directions and always would be.

Ingrid tried to keep Joel out of her mind, but all week the TV news reported the latest update on the Canelli trial. All of the participants, including Canelli himself, were viewed getting in and out of cars, leaving and entering buildings, signing papers and waving to crowds. Occasionally Ingrid would catch a glimpse of someone at Canelli's side, but it wasn't Joel. In fact, his name wasn't even mentioned. Odd, she thought. It wasn't like Joel, or Carmichael, to miss an opportunity for publicity. Probably they had a good reason for keeping a low profile. Still, it was strange.

Laura, who had a sixth sense when it came to love affairs, past, present and future, was also blessed with an insatiable curiosity. By prodding gently, but very firmly, she finally managed to wrangle an explanation of the status quo of the Christian/Stires affair. As briefly as possible, Ingrid explained that she and Joel were simply no longer interested in each other. She didn't go into the particulars, but she didn't have to. Despite her meddling, Laura knew when to back off. She was sympathetic, understanding and consoling and, to Ingrid's relief, she didn't keep prying or even offer advice, until the day of the seminar.

"What do you mean, you're not going?" Laura asked, stunned.

Ingrid wasn't swayed by Laura's theatrics. "Just what I said. I'm not interested in the criminal mind. My field is art, not law, and I refuse to sit and listen to a long, boring dissertation on a subject that doesn't concern me."

"You don't have to stay for the whole thing. No one does," Laura argued. "But the last two rows on the main floor have been reserved for the faculty. It wouldn't look good if none of us showed up, now would it?"

"I'm afraid someone else is going to have to do the showing this time."

"But, Ingrid," Laura persisted. "How do you think

it's going to look if you don't go? Everyone on the faculty knows the great Joel Stires spent that blizzard weekend at your house. If you don't show, it's going to look as if you two didn't get along."

"And we didn't. What's wrong with that?"

"Everything! Even creaky old Dean Effinger knows of such a thing as sexual chemistry. If there wasn't anything between you two—and that's what we want him to think, right?—then you'd undoubtedly attend the seminar out of respect and obligation to your guest as well as your school. But if you don't go," she lowered her voice meaningfully, "people might think you two had a quarrel."

"And they'd be right."

Laura sighed patiently. "Be reasonable. What kind of a quarrel would a beautiful, single woman and a handsome, single man who spent a weekend together have? A lover's quarrel. What else?"

"But that's not necessarily true. It could have been over anything."

"I know that. And you know that. And we both know no one will believe one word of it."

On the eve of the seminar, Ingrid argued with herself all night before finally deciding she'd go. She'd just put in an appearance, listen to the opening address and slip out unnoticed during the first hour. By so doing she would squash any possible rumors that might be going around. She owed it to Mount Traver. It was the least she could do. Joel had nothing to do with it. They had parted—one swift, clean break—and she had no desire to see him again. Never. Ever. Not even from a distance. Not even for one last time.

"Liar," she scoffed.

Dressing in a white wool skirt with a matching sweater, Ingrid relieved the monotony of the outfit with an elaborate Indian necklace of intricately woven colored beads. She not only looked elegantly chic but uniquely artistic, a characteristic that was evident in everything she wore. Hurrying through a quick breakfast, she didn't even bother to look outside at the weather. It wasn't until she stepped out the door in her high-heeled boots and fawn and beige wool coat that she realized it had snowed again during the night. Almost two inches had accumulated, and it was still coming down. Funny, she thought as she walked out to the barn to get her car, she would always think of Joel when it snowed; his square, determined face, his deep-set azure eyes, his winning smile and teasing laugh. She could almost see him now as he helped her carry the grain and hay to the feeding stations and stood and watched while she filled the bird feeders and spread the hay for the deer. But enough of that, she admonished herself. First thing she knew, she'd be blubbering again.

At the last minute Ingrid reluctantly decided to take the truck. She hated driving it in a tight skirt and high heels, but if the snow kept up, she might have trouble keeping the Corvette on the road. Better safe than sorry, she mumbled to herself as she stepped up into the truck. Backing it out of the barn, she started down the driveway and was just pulling out into the road when she caught sight of something black and white moving in the underbrush. She couldn't be sure, but she thought she detected a pair of long, fluffy tails.

Oh, hell, she thought, they're out looking for food again, and they'll probably be snooping around the barn. Ingrid hadn't seen them since the day she and Joel had stood together like two statues, waiting until the skunks released them. She remembered what a beautiful day it had been, and how the sun had glistened in Joel's eyes and how they'd gone inside and cuddled together in the living room. Joel had told her he loved her and she had . . . but enough reminiscing, she scolded herself. That was a long time ago, or at least it *seemed* long ago.

The parking lot was almost full, as students as well as local citizens crowded into the university auditorium to hear the renowned Joel Stires. She saw the TV camera crew from WHS, plus many local reporters with elaborate flash units draped around their necks. Despite Ingrid's reluctance to come, she was glad now that she had. The whole atmosphere was charged with electricity, bustling with an excitement she'd never seen at Mount Traver before. It made her feel good to be a part of it. Maybe she'd even sit through the whole seminar.

Just to be on the safe side, however, Ingrid took a seat near the end of the row, with easy access to the door. Laura came in, and Peter, and several other teachers she knew well. They were all in a light bantering mood, laughing and chatting. All except

Ingrid. Her body was so tense, she began to feel numb. *You should have stayed home, you idiot,* she chided herself. But it was too late to escape. Dean Effinger was approaching the podium.

Sitting back in her chair, Ingrid tried to concentrate, but her mind wandered during the usual opening remarks. Then suddenly she snapped to attention.

"Therefore," Dean Effinger went on, "Mr. Joel Stires will not be able to be with us today due to a prior commitment. In his place is William Cummings, also from the firm of Carmichael and Brenhoun, whose topic 'The Criminal Environment,' has been hailed as one of the finest . . ."

Ingrid didn't hear the rest. Joel wasn't here. She wouldn't see him today. She wouldn't see him any day, ever. Prior commitment? She doubted that. He was just making sure they wouldn't bump into each other ever again, not that she blamed him.

Actually, he was doing them both a favor by staying away. Not only did it avoid an embarrassing encounter, but she would be spared having to listen to him expound on the rewards of rescuing the innocent from the jaws of corrupt authorities who were more interested in their political advancement than they were in justice. The same old spiel. If she'd had to sit through the whole thing, she'd have probably gotten a headache that would have lasted a week.

Ingrid was so tense that she hardly realized that she was allowing her rebellious emotions to get out of control. All she was aware of at that moment was a strange, suffocating sense of confinement. Claustrophobia in a huge auditorium? It didn't seem possible, yet she knew she had to get out of there. She watched for her chance, feeling like a convict who was planning a prison break.

The president of the college was introduced and, finally, the speaker, who was a nice-looking man, smooth-talking, suave, had a lot of charisma. If he toed the line and did everything Carmichael told him to do, he might be as famous as Joel one day, she thought bitterly. As soon as he stopped a moment to clear his throat and take a sip of water, Ingrid slipped out of her seat, pushed through the wide double doors and bolted out of the auditorium.

Chapter Fourteen

Clutching her coat in one arm and her purse and gloves in the other, Ingrid headed for the only bench in the now deserted foyer. She noticed someone had left their coat folded on the seat. Did it look familiar? She was just ready to set her purse down when she was startled by a voice behind her.

"God, it's about time you got here."

Ingrid's eyes blinked wide with surprise and a sudden feeling of elation. Not only was the voice pleasantly familiar, but it triggered a response in her that started deep in the pit of her stomach. Only Joel could make her pulse race like that, but Ingrid refused to give in to it. Despite the tingling currents racing through her, she knew she could handle this. She'd had a week to cool off. She was more sure of herself, had a stronger guard up now. No problem.

Besides, she wondered, what was he doing here? Had he come back just to intimidate her? Coolly, she lifted her chin. "You're lucky I got here at all," she retorted. But for some reason, the words didn't have the snap she'd intended. Besides, she felt a little confused. Was there something vaguely familiar about this scene?

Turning, she watched as Joel strode toward her, tall and elegant in his gray sharkskin suit and multistriped tie, looking more devastatingly handsome than she'd ever seen him. Coming up to her side, he stood purposely closer to her than was necessary. Ingrid recognized the ploy, but she refused to back away even though his nearness had already brought a warm tingle to her depths. This time, however, she wasn't going to allow herself to succumb to his charm; not now, not ever.

When he didn't say anything, just stood there looking at her with that wicked glint of amusement in his eyes that she knew so well, she swallowed tightly and cleared her throat.

"I'm surprised to see you here," she observed calmly. "They told us you had a prior commitment."

His brows drew together in a thoughtful frown. "As a matter of fact, I do, in a way." Taking her coat, he held it for her, an absent gesture she was sure, but a disturbing one as well. It made her pulse skitter a little.

"As long as you're here, why aren't you conducting the seminar?" she asked, turning slightly so that her back was to him. But even then she could feel the tingling warmth of his presence.

"Because Carmichael has decided—put your arms in here, will you?—to promote Cummings, who is a very intelligent up-and-coming lawyer. What are you doing?"

"I'm transferring my things to the other hand, that's what I'm doing. Don't be so impatient."

"I'm not impatient, but how long does it take you to transfer a pocketbook and a pair of gloves to the other hand, for crying out loud?"

"I'm also trying to hold down the sleeves of my sweater, in case you haven't noticed."

"Oh, I've noticed, all right." His voice was not only low and seductive, but it was close to her ear. She could feel his face brushing against her hair, an exquisite sensation that sent her spirits soaring. "You look terrific, Ingrid," Joel whispered softly.

She inclined her head in a small gesture of thanks, not trusting herself to speak. The way he murmured her name was like a caress.

"In fact, I think everything about you is pretty terrific."

"Thank you," she said, heat stealing into her face. He had charm, no disputing that.

"And I'm still holding your coat," he reminded her patiently.

"Oh? Oh, yes."

"Look, why don't you set your things down on the bench, then catch your sleeves with your hands and . . . oops, what's this? Your scarf?" As he bent over to pick it up, his head bumped into her derriere. And it wasn't a little bump, either. Ingrid turned around to face him just as he straightened up and handed her the scarf with a sheepish smile. "Pardon me," he murmured.

"It's all right." But it wasn't all right. Swells of tingling excitement were beginning to rush through her. She swallowed thickly, trying to convince Joel as well as herself that his touch didn't send streamers of warmth through her, that she wasn't affected by his nearness, that there were no familiar sensations in her nerve endings. Unfortunately, she wasn't succeeding, and they both knew it.

Joel's blue eyes clung to hers for a long moment as they stood there, looking deep into each other's eyes. Ingrid was the first to pull her glance away.

Quickly, she took the scarf and purse and, dropping them on the bench, she caught the cuffs of her sweater in her hands. Turning her back to Joel once again, she reached into the sleeves of her coat. He lifted it onto her shoulders, fussed a little with the collar and then circled his arms around her neck, pressing his cheek against hers. She could feel the breath go out of him as he closed his eyes and held her tight. God, he felt good.

"I love you, Ingrid," he whispered huskily.

Her heart leaped with a response she was powerless to control. With tears springing into her eyes, she clasped her hands over his. "I love you, too," she said, her voice barely audible. "I always will."

Turning her to face him, Joel framed her face with his hands. Then, slowly, his lips descended to meet hers in a tender, loving kiss that instantly swept away all the doubts and shadows between them. Ingrid felt absolutely intoxicated with joy, and wrapping her arms around the solid strength of his body, she pulled him closer. Locking her hands behind his back, she pressed herself into the sweet tenderness of his embrace. She'd been a fool to think she could ever let him go. He was a part of her, this magnificent man in her arms. To hell with their differing opinions about values. What really mattered was the closeness, the pulsing heat of their bodies and this giddy feeling of happiness. Only Joel could bring her a total sense of completeness.

They parted, but only by a few inches. Then, slowly, Joel's mouth widened into that irresistibly sensuous smile of his. "Do you think we can make it together?"

"I know we can," she whispered.

"For richer or for poorer?"

"Absolutely."

"Because it might be a little rough going for a while, until I get started again."

She stepped back. "Started again?"

"That's right. I'm no longer with the firm of Carmichael and Brenhoun," he announced. "I'm striking out on my own."

Ingrid stared, wholly taken aback. "Am I hearing right?"

"Indeed you are. Carmichael and I had a slight falling out and I resigned."

"I can't believe it," she said. "You mean you told that old, that old . . ."

"That old man?" Joel suggested helpfully.

"You told that old man to take his marbles and go?"

"Actually, it was cocaine," he said, "but the result was the same."

"I'm surprised he let you go that easily."

"It wasn't as hard as I thought it'd be. He'd already released me from the Jalara case. And when I told him I doubted if I could get Canelli off, he decided to assign that case to someone else, too."

"He fired you?" she asked, incredulous.

"No, as a matter of fact, he left the door open. I can go back any time I want to." Gently he kissed the tip of her nose. "I thought I'd discuss it with you first."

Circling her arms around him, she locked her hands against his spine and leaned back, looking up into his eyes. "Is this a proposal?"

"You bet it is," he responded, and squeezed her to him in a big bear hug.

Smiling, she tightened her grip. "I accept."

Ingrid felt weightless in his arms as she nestled her head into his shoulder, her body fitting perfectly into his. "Have you thought of what you're going to do?" she murmured dreamily.

"I've decided to try the role of country squire and do Springland the great favor of opening an office. I'll specialize in leasehold law."

"I don't know," Ingrid murmured doubtfully. "That doesn't sound like it has enough excitement for a high-pressure personality like yours. Aren't you going to miss the excitement of criminal law?"

His voice was serious. "You know, I've given that a

lot of thought, and I've decided not to give up criminal law altogether. Surely there must be some bummers in Springland who need a good defense attorney."

"Of course there are. In fact, there was a woman on the news last night who shot her husband because he beat her up all the time, and she just lives six miles from here."

Joel's eyes snapped open. "Really? What's her name?"

Cupping his face in her hands, Ingrid reached up and kissed the tip of his nose. "It doesn't matter. You're not going to be available for consultation until after our nice, long honeymoon to some far-off place that abounds with art. Like Egypt."

"Egypt?"

"We could ride a camel to the Pyramids."

"What about Los Angeles or Chicago? We could ride a taxi to any sporting event you'd want to see."

"Italy is another trove of treasures. Almost all of Michelangelo's work is there, to say nothing of da Vinci and Raphael."

"Hawaii is having a surfing contest next month. If we hurry, we could take a few lessons."

"They say it takes three months to go through the Louvre in Paris, and even then you don't have enough time to really see it all."

A door slammed somewhere and, looking up, Ingrid saw one of her students pass through the corridor. He stopped and lifted his brows when he saw her, but tactfully hurried on his way.

Joel sighed resignedly. "I think your reputation has

just gone down the drain. What will your father say to this dastardly act?"

"My father will love it. When I went out to inspect the oil wells with him last week and told him we had broken up, he was almost as upset as I was. He had already lined up several good clients for you."

Joel nodded approvingly. "Now there's a man who thinks like I do. He doesn't believe in wasting time. Just gets right to the heart of things."

Ingrid slid him an oblique glance. "But remember, you're marrying me, not him."

"I'll try." He kissed her again. "Come on, let's get out of here. We have some thinking to do . . ."

"And vacation planning . . ."

"And a lot of other things."

Ingrid was so breathless with excitement that she thought her legs would collapse from beneath her. Reaching down, Joel grabbed his coat from the bench and shrugged into it. Then, shoving Ingrid's purse and gloves into her hands, he took her by the arm and ushered her through the door and out of the building.

It was snowing. Wrapping their arms around each other, they stood on the sidewalk and let the snowflakes fall into their faces.

"Like old times," Joel said.

"Yes," Ingrid responded quietly. She would never see snow again without thinking of Joel.

He gave her arm a nudge and, putting their heads down against the wind, they ran toward the truck, clinging to each other, reluctant to let go even for a minute.

"I'll drive," Joel announced and, without waiting for her protest, he hustled her into the passenger seat. Then he got in on the other side.

He pulled the truck to a stop at the end of the parking lot. "Which way? Right or left?"

"Right to go home, but I think we'd better stop at my mother's house first."

He looked perplexed. "Why? We've got all week to see her."

"I want her to know you're here. Then she'll tell Laura and Laura will tell everyone else, and they'll all be very discreet and not disturb us."

"Marvelous idea, but you can do that with a phone call." He turned the truck to the right. "We're headed home."

"Okay with me, but you'll have to park close to the house. Those two skunks were out looking for you this morning."

Laughing, Joel glanced at Ingrid. Her face glowed with an inner happiness he'd never seen before; her eyes sparkled with tenderness, passion and promise.

"Get out of the way, Stinky, here we come," he grinned as he headed the truck toward home.

Genuine Silhouette sterling silver bookmark for only $15.95!

What a beautiful way to hold your place in your current romance! This genuine sterling silver bookmark, with the distinctive Silhouette symbol in elegant black, measures 1½" long and 1" wide. It makes a beautiful gift for yourself, and for every romantic you know! And, at only $15.95 each, including all postage and handling charges, you'll want to order several now, while supplies last.

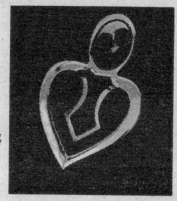

Send your name and address with check or money order for $15.95 per bookmark ordered to
Simon & Schuster Enterprises
120 Brighton Rd., P.O. Box 5020
Clifton, N.J. 07012
Attn: Bookmark

Bookmarks can be ordered pre-paid only. No charges will be accepted. Please allow 4-6 weeks for delivery.

N.Y. State Residents
Please Add Sales Tax

SBM-A

Silhouette Special Edition. Romances for the woman who expects a little more out of love.

If you enjoyed this book, and you're ready for more great romance

...get 4 romance novels FREE when you become a Silhouette Special Edition home subscriber.

Act now and we'll send you four exciting Silhouette Special Edition romance novels. They're our gift to introduce you to our convenient home subscription service. Every month, we'll send you six new passion-filled Special Edition books. Look them over for 15 days. If you keep them, pay just $11.70 for all six. Or return them at no charge.

We'll mail your books to you two full months *before they are available anywhere else.* Plus, with every shipment, you'll receive the Silhouette Books Newsletter absolutely free. *And with Silhouette Special Edition there are never any shipping or handling charges.*

Mail the coupon today to get your four free books—and more romance than you ever bargained for.

Silhouette Special Edition is a service mark and a registered trademark.

------- MAIL COUPON TODAY -------

Silhouette Special Edition℠
120 Brighton Road, P.O. Box 5084, Clifton, N.J. 07015-5084

☐ Yes, please send me FREE and without obligation, 4 exciting Silhouette Special Edition romance novels. Unless you hear from me after I receive my 4 FREE BOOKS, please send me 6 new books to preview each month. I understand that you will bill me just $1.95 each for a total of $11.70—with no additional shipping, handling or other charges. **There is no minimum number of books that I must buy, and I can cancel anytime I wish.** The first 4 books are mine to keep, even if I never take a single additional book.   **BSS2R5**

☐ Mrs.   ☐ Miss   ☐ Ms.   ☐ Mr.

Name   (please print)

Address   Apt. No.

City   State   Zip

Signature (If under 18, parent or guardian must sign.)

This offer, limited to one per customer. Terms and prices subject to change. Your enrollment is subject to acceptance by Silhouette Books.

SESE-R-A

Enjoy romance and passion, larger-than-life...

Now, thrill to 4 Silhouette Intimate Moments novels (a $9.00 value)— ABSOLUTELY FREE!

If you want more passionate sensual romance, then Silhouette Intimate Moments novels are for you!

In every 256-page book, you'll find romance that's electrifying...involving... and intense. And now, these larger-than-life romances can come into your home every month!

4 FREE books as your introduction.

Act now and we'll send you four thrilling Silhouette Intimate Moments novels. They're our gift to introduce you to our convenient home subscription service. Every month, we'll send you four new Silhouette Intimate Moments books. Look them over for 15 days. If you keep them, pay just $9.00 for all four. Or return them at no charge.

We'll mail your books to you *as soon as they are published.* Plus, with every shipment, you'll receive the Silhouette Books Newsletter absolutely free. *And Silhouette Intimate Moments is delivered free.*

Mail the coupon today and start receiving Silhouette Intimate Moments. Romance novels for women...not girls.

Silhouette Intimate Moments

Silhouette Intimate Moments™
120 Brighton Road, P.O. Box 5084, Clifton, N.J. 07015-5084

☐ **YES!** Please send me FREE and without obligation, 4 exciting Silhouette Intimate Moments romance novels. Unless you hear from me after I receive my 4 FREE books, please send 4 new Silhouette Intimate Moments novels to preview each month. I understand that you will bill me $2.25 each for a total of $9.00 — with no additional shipping, handling or other charges. **There is no minimum number of books to buy and I may cancel anytime I wish. The first 4 books are mine to keep, even if I never take a single additional book.**

☐ Mrs. ☐ Miss ☐ Ms. ☐ Mr.   BMS225

Name	(please print)	

Address		Apt. #

City ( )	State	Zip

Area Code	Telephone Number	

Signature (if under 18, parent or guardian must sign)

This offer, limited to one per customer. Terms and prices subject
to change. Your enrollment is subject to acceptance by Silhouette Books.

SILHOUETTE INSPIRATIONS is a trademark and service mark.

IM-OP-A

MAIL THIS COUPON
and get 4 thrilling

Silhouette Desire®

novels __FREE__ (a $7.80 value)

Silhouette Desire books may not be for everyone. They *are* for readers who want a sensual, provocative romance. These are modern love stories that are charged with emotion from the first page to the thrilling happy ending—about women who discover the extremes of fiery passion. Confident women who face the challenge of today's world and overcome all obstacles to attain their dreams—*and their desires.*

We believe you'll be so delighted with Silhouette Desire romance novels that you'll want to receive them regularly through our home subscription service. Your books will be *shipped to you two months before they're available anywhere else*—so you'll never miss a new title. Each month we'll send you 6 new books to look over for 15 days, without obligation. If not delighted, simply return them and owe nothing. Or keep them and pay only $1.95 each. There's no charge for postage or handling. And there's no obligation to buy anything at any time. You'll also receive a subscription to the Silhouette Books Newsletter *absolutely free!*

So don't wait. To receive your four FREE books, fill out and mail the coupon below *today!*

SILHOUETTE DESIRE and colophon are registered trademarks and a service mark.

Silhouette Desire®, 120 Brighton Road, P.O. Box 5084, Clifton, N.J. 07015-5084

Yes, please send me FREE and without obligation, 4 exciting Silhouette Desire books. Unless you hear from me after I receive them, send me 6 new Silhouette Desire books to preview each month before they're available anywhere else. I understand that you will bill me just $1.95 each for a total of $11.70—with no additional shipping, handling or other hidden charges. **There is no minimum number of books that I must buy, and I can cancel anytime I wish.** The first 4 books are mine to keep, even if I never take a single additional book.

☐ Mrs. ☐ Miss ☐ Ms. ☐ Mr.   BDS2R5

Name	*(please print)*	
Address		Apt. #
City	State	Zip
( )		
Area Code	Telephone Number	

Signature (If under 18, parent or guardian must sign.)

This offer, limited to one per customer. Terms and prices subject to change. Your enrollment is subject to acceptance by Silhouette Books.

D-OP-A